# MR. GRIMM

JORDAN QUEST FBI THRILLER SERIES BOOK 3

GARY WINSTON BROWN

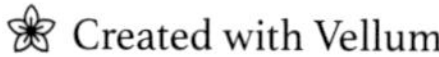
Created with Vellum

## YOUR FREE BOOK IS WAITING

As a way of saying thank you for downloading this book (or box set), I'm offering a free book when you sign up for my spam-free newsletter. You'll also be the first to hear about upcoming releases, sales, and insider information.

*JORDAN QUEST* is the prequel novella to the Jordan Quest FBI thriller series and is available exclusively to newsletter subscribers.

Visit GaryWinstonBrown.com to sign up now and get your FREE book.

*This book is dedicated to my beautiful wife, Fiona.*
*I'm lucky to have you in my life and in my corner.*

*ILYBBOBKS...ATS*

"Cruelty, like every other vice, requires no motive of itself. It only requires opportunity."

— George Eliot

# 1

DEAR COMMISSIONER HALEY,

*YOU HAVE thirty-five thousand NYPD officers at your command. There is only one of me.*

*I CAN'T IMAGINE how sad and embarrassing this has become for you.*

*HAVE you been enjoying my work?*

*I SEE you've assembled a task force to find me. Thank you. I'll send them another one soon.*

. . .

*Tic tock.*

"We've got eight more of these in evidence," Andrew Haley said. He held up the scrolls, cupped them in his hands, then opened his fingers and let them fall and scatter across his desk. "You'll want to read them all. Son of a bitch leaves one at every scene." The New York City Police Commissioner held up a red ribbon. "Ties it up with one of these, pretty as a present. Always the same condescending, holier-than-thou crap. My detectives kept the investigation off the radar until a duplicate scroll showed up on the desk of the editor-in-chief of The Times. Soon as that happened, they were all over us." Haley picked up a copy of the newspaper from his desk and handed it to the agents. "The Times printed the note. So did The Huffington Post and USA Today. They've been running articles in high rotation, all of them saying the same thing: New York's under siege... that this guy is the new Son of Sam or BTK. I'm getting calls from the Mayor's office three times a day demanding answers: Where we are with the investigation? Why haven't we made an arrest?" The Commissioner walked to his office window and stared down at the city. "We need to find this bastard," he said. "Makes me wish New York still had the goddamn death penalty."

Below, the bustling city went about its business. "Over eight million people call New York home," Haley continued. "Another sixty-million visit us each year. A serial killer who likes to brag to the press about how far ahead of us he is scares the shit out of people. And you know what happens then? Shit-scared people stay home. Which means they don't shop at Saks. Or Bloomingdale's. Or Macy's. Or thousands of other stores. They don't go out to restaurants. Since these killings hit the press, the city's economy has sunk to the bottom of the Hudson in Titanic proportions. And politicians, like Mayor Scullia, don't take too kindly to that."

Haley walked back to his desk. "I need your help. More to the point, the people of New York need your help. Personally, I don't go in for this whole psychic thing. But your reputation precedes you, Agent Quest. Same goes for you, Agent Hanover."

Jordan Quest sat in a guest chair beside her partner. Chris Hanover picked up the paper scroll and examined it in the light. The note had been written in calligraphy. Swirling, sweeping strokes of red ink graced the page.

Hanover traced his finger across the surface of the paper. "It feels old," he said. "What do we know about it?"

"Forensics says the parchment is handmade," the Commissioner replied. "Which makes it damn near impossible to trace. The ribbon is at least a hundred years old. Hasn't been manufactured for decades."

"May I see it?" Jordan asked.

Chris passed his partner the scroll. Contact with the paper brought with it a flood of images.

"Many victims," Jordan said.

"You can see that?" Commissioner Haley asked, "Just by touching the paper?"

"Yes," Jordan replied. "He's been killing for a very long time. Strange that he hasn't come to the attention of the NYPD or the Bureau until now. And this isn't ink. It's blood. Human blood. And not from a single contributor. I'd say ten... maybe more."

Commissioner Haley leaned back in his chair, folded him arms and grinned. The look was pompous, condescending. "I held back the blood information on purpose," he said to Jordan. "I wanted to see if you'd catch it, I mean, you being *psychic* and all."

Jordan dropped the note on the desk and glared at the police commissioner. “Are you serious?” she asked.

Haley leaned forward. “Watch your tone, Agent Quest. Let me remind you the FBI is here at *my* invitation.”

Jordan stood and stared down the commissioner “Not anymore. You have a serial killer on your hands. I’ve just confirmed it. Which makes it a federal case now. And let me remind *you* this isn’t my first case. I’ve been working with police agencies across the country since I was a child. So, if you or any of your people insist on testing me for your personal amusement or are holding back information which is pertinent to this investigation, let me know right now. Agent Hanover and I will be on the next plane out of here. But not before I’ve placed a call to the Attorney General’s office.” Jordan slung her purse over her shoulder. Chris stood. The agents turned to leave. “Those are my terms, Commissioner,” Jordan said. “Take them or leave them. It’s your call. Make it now.”

Haley grinned. He turned to Chris Hanover. “Is she always such a hard ass?”

Chris shared Jordan’s anger, supported his partner, said nothing.

“We’re waiting,” Jordan said.

“Okay, okay. Fair enough. I apologize, Agent Quest. You’ll get all the cooperation you need from this office. And the NYPD.” Haley extended his hand.

Jordan accepted the handshake, then held his hand. The Commissioner slowly drew it back. “What are you doing?” Haley asked. “Reading my mind or something?”

Jordan smirked. “Or something.”

Haley’s face flushed. “Well, in future... don’t.”

Chris picked up one of the scrolls from the Commissioners desk. "Mind if I hang on to this?" he asked. "I'd like Quantico to have a look at it."

"No problem." Haley opened his desk drawer, removed an evidence bag, labeled it accordingly and dropped the scroll into the bag. "We'll transfer chain of custody over to you. Keep it as long as you need it."

"Thank you," Chris said.

Jordan and Chris left the Commissioner's office. Waiting for the elevator, Jordan said, "Funny, for a non-believer he seemed a little shaken."

Chris shook his head. "You just had to do it, didn't you?"

"Do what?"

"You know what. The whole hold-his-hand-and-freak-'em-out thing back there."

"Haley needs to know I won't be taken for granted," Jordan replied.

"I get that. And I agree," Chris replied. "So now that you've done it, I have to ask. What did you read off him?"

"He's trying hard not to let it show, but he's scared to death."

"Of?"

"Losing his job and his city to this maniac."

Hanover placed the evidence bag containing the paper scroll in his jacket pocket. "Then we better make sure that doesn't happen."

## 2

LACEY CHASTAIN LEFT the bass-thudding music, applause, and flashing bright lights behind, rushed off the stage to her dressing room, showered and quickly changed into skin-tight jeans that accentuated every curve of her perfect stripper's body. She shoved "Rihanna," her leather riding crop, and "Jackson," her favorite body stocking into her locker. She'd named the short whip after her favorite pop singer and the intimate apparel after the late president whose likeness appeared on the twenty-dollar bill, her usual tip. She dried and styled her flowing blonde mane, freshened her lipstick and makeup, dabbed a little Chanel No. 5 where she knew her client would most enjoy it, said goodnight to her fellow dancers, and hurried out of the dressing room and down the hall.

The business of exotic dancing had been very good to Lacey Chastain. A featured dancer and VIP room favorite of the Odyssey Gentlemen's Club, she rarely worked a night in which she earned less than a thousand dollars in tips. Lacey had been blessed with two enviable gifts: perfect genes, and smoldering sex appeal. Like the lavender-scented oil she massaged generously over her body during her performances, her God-given gifts had helped her slide through life, and she had learned to take full advantage of them. She had an uncanny ability to separate club patrons from their money with little more than a seductive smile and a whisper of promises and pleasures to come. Only her private clients, those with very deep pockets, won the prize.

Odyssey's head of security, Anton Moore, met her at the front door. Coach handbag slung over her shoulder and a single phone bud dangling from her ear, Lacey looked positively stunning and at least five-years older than the sophomore university student she really was.

Anton never ceased to be amazed by Lacey's ability to morph effortlessly from student to seductress. As she came around the corner he whistled. Across the parking lot, the Odyssey's private limousine driver started the car. The chauffeur-driven ride home was a perk of the job enjoyed only by featured performers like Lacey. It made her feel special.

Lacey raised her hand. "Thanks, Big Man," she said, "but I won't need the car tonight."

Anton caught the driver's attention and waved him off. He smiled. "Perfect! So that means you'll let me take you home tonight! I'm telling you Lace, I make a mean pasta primavera. Secret chicken seasoning, fresh herbs, a pinch of pepper, veggies on the side. You'll think you've died and gone to heaven. Then there's the pièce de résistance..."

Lacey smiled. "And that would be?"

"Me!"

Lacey laughed. "Somehow I can't picture that buff, six-foot-four frame of yours tearing it up in the kitchen."

Anton pointed to himself. "Just who do you think taught Jamie Oliver how to cook?"

"You're bad."

"And persistent."

"Yes, you are!"

"So why no need for a lift tonight?"

"I've got a date."

Anton crossed his arms, feigned disappointment. "Why do I feel like I've just been stood up?"

Lacey laughed. "It's not that kind of date. It's business."

Anton clued in. "Oh, I get it. *That* kind of date."

"Private party in Manhattan," Lacey said. "Said they'd pick me up in front of the club."

"Have you been there before, Lace?"

Lacey shook her head. "First time."

"You sure you're gonna be okay?"

Lacey smiled. "I'll be fine, Anton. It's sweet of you to worry about me. I appreciate it."

"You've got my number handy, right?"

"On speed dial."

"And you won't hesitate to call if you need me?"

"Not for a second."

"I'm serious, Lace. I'd drop everything to come get you."

"I know you would, sweetie. And yes, if I ever feel like I'm in over my head you'll be the first person I'll call."

"Promise?"

Lacey crossed her heart and smiled. "I promise."

Anton smiled. "That's my girl."

A silver Bentley Continental GT Coupe crested the apron of the driveway and pulled to the curb in front of the club. The driver flashed his lights three times.

"That'll be my ride," Lacey said. She smiled at Anton and waved her finger. "Come down here, good looking." The bouncer bent over. Lacey kissed him on the cheek. "Thank you for caring Anton."

The big man sighed. “You’re making a mistake, Lace.”

“What do you mean?”

“Even Jamie wouldn’t pass up one of my dinner invitations.”

Lacey laughed. “Tell you what. I’ll call you tomorrow. We’ll make plans.”

“Seriously?”

“What can I say? You’re breaking me down.”

Anton smiled. “I’m just that lovable, aren’t I?”

“Yes, you are.”

“It’ll be the best date of your life. I promise.”

“I’m sure it will be. But before you have us walking down the aisle let’s start with dinner. We’ll take it from there.”

“You’ve got it.”

“All right,” Lacey said.

The driver turned on the cabin light. He appeared to be staring at her through the heavily tinted window.

Lacey got the message. “Looks like someone’s getting impatient. I better go.”

“Okay. Be safe. And remember to…”

“… call if I need help!”

“Exactly.”

Lacey walked toward the Bentley. Anton called out after her. “Hey, Lace!”

She turned around.

“You ever see the Disney movie, *Lady and the Tramp*?”

“Yeah,” Lacey replied.

“The noodle scene in the restaurant?”

“Yeah?”

Anton smiled. “It all started with pasta!”

Lacey laughed. “You’re crazy!” She waved goodbye, opened the door, and slipped into the back seat of the Bentley.

Anton spoke to himself as he watched the car pull into the street. "Crazy? About you? Better believe it."

Lacey opened her handbag and removed the invitation. It had been left for her two days ago at the club in an envelope along with two-thousand-dollars in cash.

She untied the red ribbon, unrolled the scroll.

The paper was thick, the note handwritten, the writing the most beautiful she had ever seen. Calligraphy. Very elegant.

Lacey was excited. She had never met this client before, but he certainly knew how to start off a relationship on the right foot. Luxury car. Handwritten note. The cash. What more could she ask for? Life was good.

"Pardon me, driver?"

The driver glanced at her in the rearview mirror, then lowered the privacy screen. "Yes, miss?"

"Where exactly are we going? My invitation just says it's a private function in Manhattan."

"I'm not at liberty to say. I was told to give you this." The driver passed a box over the seat to Lacey. It was wrapped in black silk and bowed with a red ribbon.

Lacey opened the box. It contained an ornately feathered and bejeweled masquerade mask.

"It's beautiful," Lacey said.

"Your host has asked that you wear it upon your arrival. Will that be all right?"

"Oh, yes," Lacey said. She took the mask out of the box and held it against her face. She smiled. "Well," she asked the driver, "how does it look?"

The driver glanced at Lacey as the Bentley pulled away from the curb. "Better than I imagined it would," he said. He raised the privacy screen.

"Excuse me?"

Thin wisps of smoke began to drift out from within the box. Lacey coughed. "What the...?"

Seconds later she lay on the seat, unconscious.

The Bentley slowly exited the parking lot of the Odyssey Gentleman's Club.

Anton Moore waved goodbye.

# 3

OTTO SCHREIBER KEPT the door to his private workshop at the back of his shop closed. On days like today, when his condition was at its worse, even the slightest brush of air against his skin had the ability to send his body into fits of raging pain, followed by a migraine headache so severe he often considered taking his own life just to make it stop.

His doctors at Bellevue had diagnosed the condition as allodynia, the result of post-traumatic stress disorder. To Otto, it was an unwelcome souvenir of ten months spent in Iraq at the hands of the enemy. His torturers had been thorough. On a strange level, he had gained a respect for them and their ability to extract secrets from him about troop movements in the region which under normal circumstances he would never have revealed. But the techniques they used to carry out his interrogation were so simple yet effective they had to be admired. Until his capture, military interrogation was his stock in trade. No one knew better how to break down another human being than Otto Schreiber.

He recalled the crude torture device they had used which was comprised of six bamboo shafts strung together with barbed-wire and wrapped tightly around his body, pinning his arms to his sides, wholly impairing his mobility. The snare, when stood on end, suspended him a foot off the ground and held him in place. Left confined in the intelligence-gathering kill house for hours at a time, gravity conspired with the razor-sharp steel barbs of the device to carve hundreds of tiny cuts deep into his skin. To say the macabre contraption was an effective interrogation tool would be an understatement.

The opportunity for escape came in an instant. As a thank you for his cooperation and telling them what they needed to know, Mohammed, Otto's lead interrogator, instructed his associates to remove him from his enclosure so that he might enjoy a hot meal and a sponge bath; two concessions he would never have offered a prisoner. Now free of the device, while enjoying the bland soup and stale bread, Otto spied the business end of a Kalashnikov assault rifle hidden beneath a prayer mat. Not knowing if the weapon was loaded, he took a chance. Feigning illness, he told Mohammed he was going to be sick. As Mohammed stepped back Otto fell forward onto the mat. He lay on his side on the ground, his back to Mohammed, clutching his stomach, writhing in apparent pain. In fact, he was clambering for the weapon. He threw back the mat, raised the gun, and pulled the trigger.

The weapon responded with deadly force.

Otto rose to his feet and delivered round after round, dispatching his captors into the afterlife, then made good his escape, shuffling from the kill house for one-and-a-half miles, one painful step after another, until finally he collapsed. His last memory of that night was the sight of the

Blackhawk helicopter hovering above him and watching the Navy SEAL's sent to rescue him fast-rope to the ground, take up positions, surround him, secure their package and ex filtrate him to Combat Outpost Callahan in Baghdad. Following an extended period of rest and recovery, Otto was deemed to be psychologically unstable, no longer able to serve his country, and discharged. Back in the United States, now a civilian, he returned to his first love, books. In particular, restoring them back to their former glory.

To Otto, rare books were a thing of beauty. He loved everything about the process of restoration. The feel of the paper in his hands. The suppleness and musty smell of the centuries-worn leather. Even the mechanically typeset letters on the page, each manually arranged to form words into sentences, sentences into paragraphs, paragraphs into pages, pages into chapters, and chapters into literary works of art. The project set out on the workbench before him was a seventeenth-century bible. Otto had deconstructed the book, removed its pages from its cover, and begun the first part of the process: re-building the cover. He rose from his desk and walked to his supply cabinet, opened the drawer marked '16th Century Leathers,' removed several pieces that matched the bible and returned to his workstation. Unbeknownst to the owner, he insisted on leaving his own artistic 'signature' on each work.

He rose from his chair and walked to a cot in the corner of the room upon which he took his afternoon nap. The cot sat on an area rug he obtained from an Iraqi businessman. He purchased the item because it reminded him of the prayer mat under which he had retrieved the assault rifle and secured his escape from captivity. Lag bolts secured the metal legs of the cot through the rug and into the wooden floor. A secret lever under the bed frame released the locks that held the cot in place. Otto pulled the lever. With a click the false floor under the cot released. The bed lifted several inches up off the floor.

The raised cot exposed a staircase that led down to Otto's special place.

In the dungeon below, a woman lay on a medical gurney, unaware of his presence due to the potent anesthetic coursing through her bloodstream.

Otto examined her naked body, located the specific section of skin he wanted for this current restoration project, cut off the flesh and held it up to the light.

Perfect.

With great reverence he lay it on a stainless-steel tray beside her.

Soon he would treat the skin with his special formulation and allow it to cure. When it was ready, he would incorporate it into the restoration of the bible.

Like the book, the girl would become a part of history, never to be forgotten.

## 4

THE FOLLOWING MORNING Jordan and Chris stepped out of the fifth-floor elevator and into the beehive of activity that was the Scroll Killer Task Force. A heated debate was taking place at the back of the room. Two of NYPD's best homicide detectives, Rick Pallister and David Keon, watched them cross the floor. Jordan read Pallister's lips as he whispered to his partner: '*Feds.*'

Chris spoke to the men. "Care to bring us up to speed, guys?" Keon crossed his arms. Pallister turned away. The detectives remained closed, stoic.

"Let me guess," Jordan said. "You two must be the welcoming committee."

A voice boomed from across the room, gruff, deep and none too happy with what he was seeing. "Is there a problem here?"

Pallister turned around. "No, sir."

Keon shook his head. "We're good."

The big man crossed the floor. Jordan and Chris' New York bureau liaison, FBI Special Agent Max Penner, slapped

Pallister on the shoulder and tightened his grip in a not-so-friendly manner. "I didn't think so," Penner said. Pallister tried not to wince under Penner's iron grasp. No luck. Penner's hand engulfed the detective's shoulder. At six-foot-two, the agent appeared to be carved from a slab of muscle and bone. The sleeve-tattoos on his arm peeked out from under the French cuff of his crisp white dress shirt. The garment strained as he flexed his powerful shoulders.

"I expect you'll be extending every courtesy to my new friends here. Or would you prefer I take the matter of your disinterest to cooperate up with your boss?" Penner was referring to Police Commissioner Haley.

"That won't be necessary," Keon said. He shook hands with Jordan and Chris. "Welcome to the jungle, agents. I hope you've had your shots."

Pallister qualified Keon's remark. "You'll understand what Detective Keon means by that after you've had a closer look at the board. Whoever the Scroll Killer is one thing is certain. He, or she, is a goddamn animal."

"Give me the room," Agent Penner said. "I'll fill in Agents Quest and Hanover. You two head downstairs. Bring up everything we've got on SK. I want Agent Quest to look over all the evidence we've collected and give me her opinion."

Keon spoke. "What do we look like, Penner? Your..."

Pallister cut off his partner mid-sentence. "We'll be happy to," he said. "It's our pleasure to assist the FBI any way that we can."

"Right answer," Penner replied.

Penner watched the detectives walk away. Keon muttered to himself. Pallister opted to say nothing, kept walking.

"You have no idea how much I dislike that little prime-time prick," Penner said.

"Keon?" Chris asked.

Penner nodded. "Guy's been a royal pain in my ass since the Bureau got involved with the case. Guess he figured he would make his career on this one. Ask me, he's done nothing but spin his wheels. The man needs to be reminded he works for the *victim*. I've never met such a goddamn glory hound. If there's a television camera within a block of the scene you can bet your ass it'll be his mug you'll see on the six o'clock news. Probably carries a makeup kit with him wherever he goes. Moron."

Chris laughed. "Tell me how you really feel, Agent Penner."

Penner smiled. "Call me Max. Sorry, I don't tolerate bureaucrat bullshit or case jumpers very well," he admitted. "Two years in deep cover will do that to you. I thought I'd seen it all with bike gangs. But Scroll takes the cake. Keon was right. He is one sick sonofabitch." He pointed to the board. "See for yourself."

Penner directed Jordan and Chris' attention to a large tack board which ran the full width of the Scroll Killer Task Force room. Crime scene photos depicting the remains of twenty victims were taped to the board, organized in chronological order, starting from the date the first body had been found.

"Anything strike you as unusual?" Penner asked.

Jordan nodded. "No notes, no stickies... not a single thing to show that progress is being made on the case."

"Precisely," Penner said. "Every single victim was killed in a different manner and a different means was employed to do so. The only common connections are the damn scrolls found with the bodies. Beyond that, victimology is all over the map. We can't find one cohesive connection that marries one vic to another. We're up to twenty so far. All appear to be unrelated. This guy doesn't even have a particular type. He's not just targeting blondes or brunettes, married or single. We've got Caucasian, African American, Latino, Asian, soccer moms, hookers, businesswomen, slim, heavy. Ironically, the only thing that stands out is how uniquely different each murder is to the next. If it were not for the scrolls being left at every murder scene, I'd say we were looking for twenty different killers."

"A team of serial killers... all working together? That would be insane," Chris said.

"Aptly put," Penner stated. He stepped back from the board, reviewed the wall. "In my twenty years on the job I've never seen anything like it."

"No men," Jordan said.

"Say what?" Penner asked.

"There are no male victims, nor couples. Just women. Considering the inconsistencies that could be significant."

"Agreed," Penner said.

The elevator doors opened. Pallister and Keon returned, each pushing a supply cart full of file boxes marked 'SK EVIDENCE.'

"Here you go, your highness," Keon said to Agent Penner. "Twenty boxes. One for each vic." He turned to Jordan and Chris. "Knock yourselves out."

Jordan immediately zeroed in on the aura surrounding one particular box on Pallister's cart.

The evidence label read, "Courtney Valentine."

"This one," she said. "This is where we start."

She pulled the box off the cart, placed it on a desk, broke the evidence seal, and removed the lid.

The psychic impression she received from its contents struck her hard.

"This was bad," Jordan said. "Real bad."

# 5

ON WAKING, LACEY Chastain's mind processed her predicament within seconds, then manifested the appropriate response with a scream.

She struggled in the rope and pulley system which supported her, hands tied behind her back, feet bound, body swaying from side-to-side in a slow, steady arc. She saw the man sitting in the corner, an open leather-bound book in his lap, head slumped forward, fast asleep. Oddly, her cries did not startle him out of his deep slumber. He merely opened his eyes, blinked twice, lifted his head, smiled, and said, "Good morning, Lacey."

Lacey pulled and kicked at the ropes, then yelled at the top of her lungs. "Who the hell are you? Let me go, you sonofabitch!"

Otto Schreiber stood, removed his wire-rimmed glasses, closed the book, placed it on the stool and calmly said, "Do it again."

"Do what?"

"Yell." He walked behind her and tested the security of

the lifting rope secured to her wrist. "As loud as you want, for as long as you want."

Lacey cried out. The pain in her shoulder sockets was unimaginable. How long had she been unconscious, suspended there? All night?

Schreiber circled her, then faced her. "You're a student, Lacey. Am I right? Between dances and dates that is. How up are you on eighteenth century history? The Inquisition, in particular?"

"I'm in no fucking mood for a history lesson, asshole," Lacey spat out. She tried unsuccessfully to mask the fear in her voice. "Let me go!"

Schreiber shrugged, then continued. He motioned at the contraption that bound her. "This device is called a strappado," he said. "Let me show you how it works."

He pulled down hard on the lifting rope behind her back. Lacey felt her feet pull out from under her. Her body fell forward, dropped hard, her shoulders bearing her full weight. The pain was immediate, agonizing, extreme, white-hot. She danced with darkness but remained conscious.

"This was the preferred method of torture of the day," Schreiber said, "used to elicit a confession from the accused. Do you have something you need to confess, Lacey? A crime you have committed, perhaps? A secret you need to reveal?"

Lacey watched a fine strand of spittle leave her mouth, travel down, and touch the floor. "What are you talking about? I have no secrets."

"Oh, come now," Schreiber said. "We all have something hidden away. A dark memory from our past, something we've said or done that we wish we could take back."

"You mean like getting into the car with you?"

Schreiber pulled hard on the rope. With an audible *click*, Lacey heard her arms dislocate from their sockets.

This time the pain proved too much to bear. She offered no scream, no cry, no plea for mercy. Darkness enveloped her.

Lacey fainted.

Schreiber stared at the young woman for a while, head fallen, spit-string anchoring her head to the floor. He took a moment to revel in her exquisite beauty.

He had made a perfect choice.

She would make a perfect wife.

There would be festivities, a celebration, bridesmaids. As always, the streets would provide.

He called out. "I'd like you all to meet Lacey, my future wife. You will do whatever she says, act on her every whim. Is that understood?"

An attack of voices assaulted him from the surrounding cells that ran the length of the dungeon.

"Stop hurting her!"

"Leave her alone, you bastard!"

"Let the rest of the girls go. Take me instead."

"Why are you doing this to us?"

"You have no right!"

"Burn in hell, you psychopath!"

"Please, let me go. I want to go home."

"She'd rather die than marry you!"

"Freak!"

"SILENCE!" Schreiber called out. One woman cried softly. Another chastised her, told her to pull herself together. The whimpering ceased.

The woman on the operating table moaned.

The sedative was wearing off.

Schreiber tended to her open wound and evaluated the sample layer of skin he had earlier sectioned from her body. The thickness was exact, the size ideal.

He retrieved the book from the stool and placed the skin between its pages.

When dry it would make an excellent writing surface.

Paper scrolls no longer interested him. Human flesh would make the delivery of his messages much more compelling to read.

Schreiber spoke to his captives. “Let this be a lesson to you all. I will not be disobeyed. A price will be paid for insubordination.”

He listened, awaited a reply.

The chamber had fallen mouse quiet.

## 6

JORDAN SHUDDERED AS the psychic vision that was the abduction and horrific murder of Courtney Valentine played out in her mind.

The young pediatric nurse, having finished her shift at St. Christopher's Hospital, had been driving home from downtown Brooklyn when her nearly new four-wheel drive suddenly began to cough and sputter, forcing her to pull on to a service road leading into an apartment complex under construction. It had been a harrowing day for Courtney from the moment she had walked through the doors of the neonatal intensive care unit and into the ward. She and her team had spent the afternoon fighting to save the life of young Thomas Masterson, the three-day-old son of United States Senator Allan Masterson and his wife, Tracey. Thomas, the Masterson's only surviving triplet, had been born with spina bifida. His younger siblings, brother Caleb and sister Ann, also born physically challenged, were not as strong as their older brother and took their final breaths fifteen-minutes apart after entering the world. Angry at God for claiming their two precious children, the

Masterson's placed what little faith they had left in the Divine and begged for a miracle that would save Thomas' life. The child succumbed to the insidious disease. The Masterson's were inconsolable and took no solace from the nursing staff when talk turned to their children serving a higher purpose than what was intended for them in this world. Tracey Masterson had to be removed from the unit by security personnel. No one blamed her for her sudden and complete mental and emotional breakdown, but her attempt to leave the hospital with her three dead children bundled haplessly in her arms could not be permitted. Hearing of the incident, Courtney and her team took turns excusing themselves to the staff room and crying until they could cry no more, then collected themselves and returned to the ward, ready to save the life of the next precious child that demanded their attention. Never had Courtney been more ready to end a day than she was at that moment.

Cursing the vehicle malfunction when all she wanted to do was to drive home, pour herself a glass of cabernet sauvignon and draw a steaming hot bath, she popped the hood, stepped out of the car, and examined the engine, having absolutely no clue as to the source of the problem or how to fix it. She was grateful when, moments later, a silver Bentley limousine pulled in behind her, turned on its four-way flashers and the driver stepped out and asked if he could be of assistance.

Jordan turned Courtney's bloodied and shredded nursing smock in her hands. In doing so, the scene changed. The man had insisted that Courtney wait in the back of the limo while he inspected her vehicle, said it was he least he could do to make the end of her day more comfortable, and that she should help herself to the open bar. Guard down, overcome by the emotional trauma of the day, Courtney readily accepted. It surprised her how quickly she became impaired by the small amount of alcohol she had consumed. When the man returned to the limo she had already passed out. Which is what he had expected. He had laced the alcohol with his special concoction of potent drugs. Unconscious, he pulled her out of the back seat of the car and dragged her behind the blowing plastic sheets in the apartment complex that separated one unfinished room from the next, then turned on a concrete-cutting circular saw and cut her body into pieces.

"Jesus," Jordan said.

"What did you see?" Chris asked.

"Courtney was still alive at the time of her death. Drugged, wholly incapacitated, but alive."

"You saw that?" Agent Penner asked.

"And more," Jordan answered. "Where did you find the remains?"

"The Blakey-Chadd Projects," Penner said. "In garbage bags. Which doesn't surprise me if you know the BCP area like I do. Drugs and gangs. The area's polluted with them. The medical examiner said she had enough legal and illegal drugs in her system to kill her twice over. But chopping up the body? That's overkill if ever I've seen it. Even for the lowlife that prey on their junkie customers."

"Courtney wasn't a junkie. She was a nurse. And she wasn't killed there."

"Then where?" Chris asked.

"A construction site."

Penner crossed his arms. "You're gonna have to do better than that Agent Quest. Construction site? This is New York City. There isn't a block for miles around that isn't under construction."

"Then I'll make it easy for you," Jordan replied.

"How's that?" Penner asked.

"Find the one with the blood-soaked concrete saw. That's your crime scene. And one more thing. Have your pals Pallister and Keon put together a list of limousine companies in the city."

"Why?"

"The Scroll Killer likes to travel well."

Chris and Penner exchanged glances. "He has a driver?" Chris asked.

"He *is* the driver," Jordan replied.

## 7

ANTON MOORE RAPPED on the door to the dancers dressing room and called out. "It's Anton. Okay if I come in?"

Shona-Lee Cairns called out. "Thank you for asking, sweetie. Yeah, you can come in."

Anton opened the door and walked inside. Shona-Lee sat in front of her make-up mirror applying her lipstick. Several of the opening acts dusted their bodies with stage powder, rendering their physical appearance as near to perfection as any club patron could imagine. The Odyssey had a reputation for delivering quality talent to its guests and that included Shona-Lee. Her perfect body shimmered in the light of the room.

"You're looking beautiful tonight," Anton said as he entered the room.

Shona smiled. "Flattery will get you everywhere," she replied.

Anton laughed. "Anyone seen Lacey?" he asked.

The women shook their heads.

"Everything all right, honey?" Shona-Lee asked.

"I suppose so," Anton replied. "Russ asked me to check. He wants her to work a double today. She's not answering her cell phone. He left a message for her last night and another again this morning. Nothing. That's unusual for her."

Russ Paley, the club's owner, took great pride in assuring his dancers safe transportation to and from the club. Mike Degario drove the club's limousine.

"You talk to Mike?" Shona-Lee asked. "He would have driven her home."

Anton shook his head. "Not last night. Lacey had a private function."

"She likes to party with the high-rollers," Shona-Lee said. "Who wouldn't?"

A look of deep concern was etched on Anton's face. "I've warned her about these dates," he said. "She should stick to the club. We can control what happens here. Out there the rules don't apply."

Shona-Lee put down her lip gloss. "You're really worried about her, aren't you?"

Anton nodded. "Something doesn't feel right."

"Have you checked her apartment? Maybe she partied a little too hard last night, got in late, slept in."

"I don't have her address. Besides, Russ didn't suggest I do a wellness check."

"Screw Russ," Shona-Lee said. "This is Lacey-who-wouldn't-hurt-a-fly we're talking about." The dancer walked to her locker, took out her purse, removed her cellphone and pulled up Lacey's contact information. "112 St. Regis Court, Brooklyn. Apartment 3-B."

Anton punched the information into his phone. "Got it. Thanks."

Shona-Lee handed Anton the spare apartment key

Lacey had given her. "The security keypad is in the closet on your left. Pass code is 41062. When you find her tell her she's totally pissed me off," she said. "Lacey knows the pro-dating rules: always call your back-up buddy before a date with the deets on where you'll be, with whom and for how long. No exceptions. I'm her BB and she's mine. She never called." Shona-Lee suddenly sounded scared. "Jesus, Anton. Now you've got me worried too."

"Forget about it. I'm sure everything is fine," Anton said. "I'm probably overreacting. Like you say, she messed up, forgot the rules."

"Lacey forget? Not a chance. She's whip-smart and as self-disciplined as they come. The girl doesn't forget a damn thing. Unlike the rest of us she doesn't need this gig. She's got another six months to go, then she's out of the business altogether."

"I didn't know she was planning on leaving," Anton said.

Shona-Lee nodded. "This was never her long-term plan. She wanted to make enough money to pay for her education and set herself up in practice after she graduated."

"Practice?"

"She's going to be a psychologist. Lacey's all about helping people. Like I said, she wouldn't hurt a fly."

Anton turned to leave. There was an urgent tone in his voice. "I'll tell her to call you as soon as I find her."

"She better."

FOUR THREE-STORY BROWNSTONES on the north end of Nostrand Avenue in Brooklyn comprised the St. Regis Court apartment complex. Unlike other buildings in the neighborhood its walls were free of graffiti. No overflowing trash cans or discarded household items lined its driveways.

Like Lacey, the residences bore an air of subtle sophistication.

Anton removed the apartment key from his pocket, opened the main door, then rode the elevator to the third floor. The door to Lacey's apartment was the second on the left. He slipped the key into the lock, turned the knob, and opened the door.

No security chain snapped tight to prevent him from entering, which told him Lacey was probably not at home. No *beep... beep... beep* from the security system announced its countdown. Anton checked the alarm control panel. Disabled. No single woman living alone in New York City, especially a beautiful exotic dancer like Lacey Chastain, would fail to engage the security chain on her apartment door and turn on her alarm system before retiring for the night. He knew how safety-conscious Lacey was. She was also quite capable of taking care of herself. A third-degree black belt in taekwondo, Lacey had taught her fellow dancers the basics of self-defense and never left the club without her pepper-spray in hand. Too many crazies out there, she said.

Concern made the leap to worry.

He called out. "Lacey? It's me, Anton. You home?"

No reply.

Again. "Lace?"

Being head of security for the Odyssey Gentlemen's Club and a personal security expert, Anton periodically found himself in situations that called for more than a physical response to deal with a potentially dangerous patron. He was licensed to carry a concealed weapon. Though he'd never had to present it on the job, every instinct within him cried out that something was wrong. Anton slipped his hand under his jacket and wrapped it around the Colt semiautomatic handgun fitted in the small of his back. He called out once more. "Lacey, if you're here, answer me."

All quiet.

Anton walked down the corridor and past the guest bedroom. Ahead, the door to the master bedroom was ajar. He was sure he'd seen it move.

"Lacey? That you?"

He debated whether to leave the apartment, call the police, report the suspicious circumstances, and let the authorities clear the residence. No, he thought. He had come this far. What if Lacey was in there, bound and gagged, being held against her will by a psychopath, unable to speak, or worse, unconscious? He wouldn't be able to live with himself if he failed to act right here, right now, at the time when she might need him the most.

Anton called out. "You... in the room. Step out... slowly."

The door moved.

Anton stepped ahead.

He never saw the attack coming.

Steel met bone. The blow to the back of his head dropped him to the floor.

He lost consciousness.

# 8

LACEY SLOWLY OPENED her eyes and stared at the patterns of dust and dirt on the concrete floor below. Slumped forward, head down, her body was numb from the incredible pain she had been subjected to by the barbaric torture device. She wanted to cry out, to tell the asshole anything he wanted to hear, that she would do anything he wanted her to do, be anything he wanted her to...

*Fuck that. Never going to happen.*

In her dizzying return to consciousness, she couldn't tell if the voices she heard were real or imagined. Lacey cut out the mental distractions and focused. They became real.

"Hey," she said. Her voice was weak, without power, barely audible. She closed her eyes and focused on her breathing... in... out... in... out. Slowly she drew air deeper into her lungs, powered up her body. She tried again. "Can anybody hear me?"

Her second attempt to speak, stronger than the first, met with a reply. Behind her a woman answered. "You okay?"

Lacey raised her head. Her body swayed from side to

side in the contraption. She remembered the words drilled into her through fifteen years of martial arts training... *the only enemy is fear...* and collected herself.

"I've been better," Lacey replied. "Where are we?"

"No idea," the woman said.

"How many of us are there?"

"Eight, plus the donor."

"*Donor?*"

"The girl on the table. We don't know her name. That's what he calls her."

The woman on the gurney moaned. The anesthesia was wearing off. She was coming around.

"How long has she been like that?" Lacey asked.

Another voice answered. "Two days."

"What happened?"

"She tried to run," the voice said. "We watched him. The bastard kept punching her. When she finally stopped moving, he strapped her to the table and hooked up the IV. Sometimes he'll cut off the flow and wait until she comes around, take a section of her skin while she's awake, then put her back under when she screams from the pain."

"How long have you been here?" Lacey asked.

"A week," the first woman replied.

"Ten days," said the second.

"Jesus."

"I'm Melinda," the first woman said.

"Victoria," the second said.

"I'm Lacey."

The woman on the table moaned again. Lacey's head was inches from the Velcro strap that bound her right wrist to the gurney. Despite the wrenching pain in her arm sockets, Lacey pushed off on the tips of her toes and rocked back and forth. The braided cinching rope behind her back squeaked with the momentum. The first attempt to catch a section of the Velcro band between her teeth failed. Lacey felt as if her arms were about to pull out of their sockets and tear away from her body. The second forward swinging attempt proved as unsuccessful as the first, and Lacey felt the familiar rush of darkness from which she had emerged mere moments ago returning. There was a limit to the pain her body could take.

One last try.

*The only enemy is fear.*

Lacey pushed off, threw her body forward, opened her mouth and caught a fraction of the Velcro strap between her teeth. She bit down hard and held fast to the material. Suspended in the air, the wiry plastic loops cut into her lips and gums and abraded the corners of her mouth. Lacey breathed heavily through her nose. Saliva pooled in her mouth, dripped down, soaked the strap. She refused to release her bite on the plastic strip. Tethered to both the table and the woman, Lacey saw her fingers move. As she came out of her medically induced stupor her head lolled to her right. Her eyes suddenly met Lacey's, wide with fear. She screamed and yanked her arm away.

The counter-leverage was exactly what Lacey was hoping for.

Lacey bit down, turned her head away from the struggling woman and shook the Velcro strap in her mouth like a dog attacking a play toy.

In a blind panic, the woman pulled her hand free.

As Lacey let go, gravity took over. Now untethered, her body swung back. A wave of pain fell over her. For what felt like an eternity she stared at the concrete floor, floating on a tranquil sea of semi-consciousness. It was impossible for her to move. Her arms felt as though they were on fire within her shoulder sockets. She could feel her stomach roll. The pain was too much. She was going to be sick. She was helpless and bound. And for the first time since the beginning of her ordeal, she felt the agony of defeat.

Just as Lacey prepared herself to surrender to the pain, she suddenly felt tremendous relief in her shoulders. Her body was being lowered to the ground.

The bastard had returned. Not done with her yet, he was preparing her for the next level of torture.

"Just kill me already," Lacey said. "I don't have the strength to fight back. I lost. You won. Happy?"

"No one's going to hurt you," an unfamiliar voice replied. "Least of all me."

Lacey opened her eyes. The woman from the table was kneeling beside her, holding her hand. "Think you can sit?" she asked.

Lacey smiled. "Yeah," she replied. "I think so."

"You saved my life," the woman said. She helped Lacey up. "I don't know how I can ever repay you. Thank you. I'm Bonnie. Bonnie Cole."

"Lacey," Lacey said. "Pleased to meet you, Bonnie. Do you mind if I ask a favor?"

"Anything."

"Get me the hell out of this thing."

Bonnie smiled. "You got it."

# 9

OTTO SCHREIBER HAD used Lacey's house key to let himself into her apartment. Back at his shop he had rummaged through her purse, found her pocketbook containing the residence keys, driver's license (from which he had obtained her home address), New York University student identification card, cellphone, and canister of pepper spray. He recognized the man laying at his feet as the doorman from the Odyssey Gentlemen's Club from which he had picked up Lacey last night. He had struck him from behind with enough force to knock him out cold. Otto knelt and inspected the area of impact. No blood. He checked the man's pulse. Steady. Except for a walloping headache on waking, he would be fine. If he wasn't, if his injuries proved to be greater than what his cursory examination could provide, resulting perhaps in a subdural hematoma, hydrocephalus or neurological impairment, well, too bad for him. In coming to Lacey's apartment, he had brought the problem upon himself. He should be thankful he wasn't dead although that option still wasn't off the table.

Schreiber returned the aluminum baseball bat he had used to subdue the man to the umbrella stand beside Lacey's front door, stepped over the unconscious man, and entered her bedroom. If she was to be comfortable in her new home, she would need fresh clothes and familiar items such as her favorite perfumes, soaps, makeup, hairspray, undergarments and shoes. There would be a period of adjustment, of course. Change of any kind is never easy.

Otto took a moment to reflect on his success. To date, he had kidnapped and murdered thirty women over the course of his serial killing career and evaded capture by the authorities. He didn't see it as killing as much as a 'sorting' process. In the early days of his murder spree, he applied the tradecraft he had learned during his time in the military; interrogation as an art form, and one which he had perfected. The right question, asked the right way and supported by a strong physical incentive, always elicited the desired response. The custom blend of odorless knock out gas and time-delay fuse mechanism he had designed and used to render his victim's unconscious had made the skinning process that much easier to execute. He had devised many ingenious methods to deliver the gas but the false bottom gift box with its hidden diffuser provided the best results. In his experience, no woman could resist the desire to know what treasure lay within the ornately wrapped boxes, especially when accompanied by a note handwritten by an expert calligrapher. The romantic notion of a gift being sent by an unknown admirer worked like a charm. All he had to do was observe her routine, follow her, wait until she was alone, then knock on the door and hand-deliver the box. None of his victims had taken longer than five minutes before they'd opened the gift, proving curiosity to be the bane of human nature. He would wait in the Bentley for a few minutes, then return to the domicile, deftly work the lock with his professional burglar's tools, then enter the premises to find his victim lying unconscious on the floor. If he were to elevate murder to an art form perfection was required, much like the attention he paid to his book restoration commissions. He had carefully considered every aspect of his home invasions. After locking the door, he would secure his victim, usually in her bedroom, bind and gag her, then wake her and begin the interview process. He was always polite and courteous. When one is in a state of unadulterated panic cooperation is best gained by building rapport. Gags were necessary at first, and he opted to use a piece of her clothing most of the time, usually her top. When she had stopped screaming into the gag and promised to obey, he would loosen the material, assure her he meant her no harm, and permit her to speak. He would then remove the small custom-made notebook from his pocket and ask his standard interrogation questions: *If today was your last day on Earth, how would you prefer to die? What body part would you least like to lose? On a scale of one to ten, ten being completely satisfied and one being extremely unsatisfied, how would you rate the quality of sex with your partner? Cat or dog person? Meat lover or vegan? Pop or rap?* He didn't really care what answers she gave. He had already decided she would die from the moment he had laid eyes on her. The interview made the pretext to the inevitable more intimate and enjoyable. He was equally accommodating and offered to answer her every question although they were often disappointingly few and always the same: *Why me? What are you going to do with me? Let me go. I won't tell a soul.* No, they wouldn't. He would see to that. Over time, the mechanical act of killing had lost its zeal. Now it was all about the game.

Stepping up the body count, evading capture, being smarter than his adversaries at the NYPD, pushing the envelope, daring them to catch him, reveling in their ineptitude, raising the stakes and the penultimate rush: having the God-like power and ability to take the life of another human being at will.

Otto placed the items he had come for in his knapsack, threw the bag over his shoulder, stepped over the glorified strip club doorman and walked to the front door.

Lacey would be happy. Soon she would have everything she would need to be comfortable in her new accommodations.

He would go hunting tonight. Of the ten cells he had constructed in his special place beneath the shop, only two were currently occupied. Eight were vacant, the bodies of the former occupants long since discarded in places the police had discovered, compliments of his beautifully crafted notes.

The love of his life was in the strappado. He would free her when he got back to the store, make her more comfortable. As for the others, inventory was getting low. He would need to dispose of the donor soon. She had served her purpose. In harvesting her skin, he had let the deep grafts go untreated. Of the nine excisions he had made four had become grossly infected. One appeared necrotic. This was by choice. He found the process of biological destruction and cell death fascinating to observe. He had kept impeccable notes on the progress of each victim's mental and physical degradation.

The more he thought about it the more excited and psychologically prepared he became for the hunt. It would be an amazing night.

What he was not prepared for was the bullet that tore through the knapsack, caught him squarely in his shoulder, and nearly dropped him to the ground.

# 10

COURTNEY VALENTINE'S DEATH room flashed through Jordan's mind. Construction materials lay strewn about the murder scene: sheets of drywall on wooden racks, spools of coiled electrical wire, plastic buckets filled with miscellaneous end cuts, bent nails, chunks of broken plaster and dry waste. In the middle of the room, the bloodied concrete table saw.

Sheets of plastic secured to steel studs, intended to contain the dust during the concrete cutting process, had torn away in sections. A brisk wind blew through the ground floor of the unfinished building, disturbing the area, and causing the plastic walls to rip, flap in the breeze, and snap tight like untethered sails. Energy spent, the loosed sheets fell until the next gust of wind came along and billowed them again, recharged them with life, the reanimation repeated with each new gale.

Courtney Valentine's innate life force was one of the strongest Jordan had ever experienced. She followed the route to the building as one would follow a mist that had settled over a damp road which only she could see.

Agent Max Penner was behind the wheel of the NYPD-issued Crown Victoria sedan. “You sure you know where you’re going?” he asked Jordan. “You’re not even from New York.”

“Humor me,” Jordan replied. She stared out the passenger window. The energy was becoming stronger, the mist thicker. It swirled around a distant corner. She pointed ahead. “Take a left at the next lights.”

“What is this?” Penner asked. “Some kind of psychic GPS?”

“That’s one way of putting it,” Jordan replied.

“Damn.” The agent opened his jacket pocket, fished out a cellophane packet of toothpicks, stuck one in the corner of his mouth, then passed the pack around. “Toothpick?” he asked Jordan.

Jordan smiled. “I’m not really a toothpick kind of girl.”

“They’re cinnamon.”

“Thanks, but no.”

“I have spearmint, too.”

Jordan smiled. Penner was as rough and tumble as they came. Even the simple gesture of offering her a toothpick seemed difficult for him. He passed the package over his shoulder. “Agent Hanover?”

Chris shook his head. “I’m good.”

“It’s these or cigarettes,” Penner said, “and my wife will kill me if I don’t give up the cancer sticks. Never smoked before going undercover. Never drank either. Now I could go through a forty pounder of rum and a pack of smokes for breakfast if I wanted to and still walk a straight line, no problem. Frankly, I’m surprised my liver hasn’t shriveled up and died by now. Those bikers are hard drinking bastards.”

“You said you were undercover for two years?” Chris asked.

"Two years, two months and sixteen days. That assignment took a lot out of me. How about you, Hanover? Ever work UC?"

"No," Chris answered. "There were opportunities. Undercover just wasn't for me."

"I hear ya," Penner answered. "You married?"

"Not yet," Chris replied. "Maybe one day."

"Anyone serious?"

"Working on it."

Penner chewed on the toothpick. "That's not a gig you want to take if you have a wife and family like I do. I wasn't allowed to contact my Jenny or our kids the whole time. It would have been too dangerous for them. They heard from me through my SAC. No phone calls or visits, ever. Trust me, that will tear the crap out of your heart. I broke the rules once. Couldn't help myself. I arranged a meet across the street from my daughters' school and timed the drug buy when I knew she'd be outside for recess. Told my contact we were safer meeting in public, in a school zone. I did the deal - one-hundred grand in Ecstasy - in exchange for a truckload of automatic weapons, then stole a few minutes with her when my guy left. No personal contact mind you. I just watched her for a little while. The bureau pulled me out the next morning before SWAT raided the clubhouse. They called my wife, told her I was out, and to grab the go bags she'd kept packed for us and the kids. Agents picked them up and had us on a plane to Colorado within the hour. We spent the next year and a half in Telluride until they called me to testify. We got them. Took 'em all down. Even the son of a Urabenos Columbian cartel boss. As far as I know that asshole still has a bounty on my head, except none of them really know what I look like. And that's exactly how I plan to keep it, thank you very much."

Jordan spoke to the agent. "We're close," she said.

Penner glanced at her. "You're freaking me out."

Jordan smiled. "I get that a lot."

From the back seat, Chris said, "I take it you've never worked with a psychic before?"

Penner shook his head. "Nope. This is a first for me."

"You get used it," Chris said. "I know it seems a little strange at first. It was for me, too. Just keep an open mind and remember two things."

"Namely?"

"One, that Jordan's the real deal and not some street level swami."

"Fair enough," Penner replied. "And the second?"

Jordan answered for her partner. "I'm never wrong."

Penner smiled as he turned the corner. "You and my wife both."

"There," Jordan said. "Half a block down the road. That's the building we're looking for."

The agents pulled up to the entrance of the cordoned off construction site. The sign posted at the front entrance read, CLOSED UNTIL FURTHER NOTICE. TRESPASSERS WILL BE PROSECUTED. The small print specified building code violations as the reason for the cessation of the project.

"This is where he killed Courtney Valentine," Jordan said. "Inside, on the main floor." In her mind, the plastic sheets billowed and fell. Blood dripped from the blade of the concrete saw.

Ahead, the ghostly countenance of the murdered woman acknowledged Jordan, then turned and drifted into the building.

Jordan stepped out of the car. "This way," she said.

The agents entered the murder site.

## 11

BONNIE COLE CRIED out as she helped Lacey to her feet. The raw wounds on her body cracked, pulled open, oozed. The two women leaned on each other for support.

"You all right?" Lacey asked.

"No, but I will be," Bonnie replied.

"What kind of pathetic excuse for a human being does this to another person?" Lacey said.

"The kind that I want to be as far away from as possible."

"We need to treat your wounds. I've seen injuries like this before. You could lose your arm."

"Better my arm than my life," Bonnie replied. "Getting out of here is the priority. You're more mobile than I am. Check on the others. Get them out of their cells. He keeps a medical kit in the cabinet under the stairs. I've seen him use it on one of the girls."

"All right," Lacey said. She searched the room for the keys to the cells, found none.

Melinda and Victoria's cells were adjoined. Lacey spoke to the women. "Do you know where he keeps the keys?"

"They're always with him," Melinda answered. "There's no way for us to get out of here."

"We have to try," Lacey said. She examined the door, searched for a weak point. The frame of the cell was secured to the concrete floor with lag bolts and to the wooden ceiling by heavy screws. Lacey tried shaking the frame. It wouldn't budge.

Victoria spoke as she watched the women struggle to loosen the steel door. "There's only one option," she said.

"I'm open to suggestions," Lacey replied.

"You need to get out of here. Contact the police. When they find us, they'll free us."

Melinda agreed. She tested her cell door, shook it violently. "Victoria's right. We don't have a hope in hell of getting out of here. You do. But you'll have to hurry. He's been gone half an hour. He could be back any minute."

"For all we know he's upstairs right now," Bonnie said, "listening to us on the other side of the door. Maybe he's getting ready to pump the room full of whatever that shit was he used to knock us out in the first place. Only this time he won't shut it off. Just keep it flowing until we've breathed in enough of it that our bodies can't take it anymore and we die."

"Anybody want to know what I think?" Lacey offered.

"I do," Bonnie said.

"I think you've all been through one hell of a trauma. You're terrified and not thinking straight. We need a plan. Let's start with the obvious. How often does he check on you?"

"Every day," Melinda said.

"Once a day? Twice?"

"Once," Victoria said. "In the evening, I think. I've lost

track of time. I don't even know if its day or night outside right now."

"He brings us food and water," Melinda said. "Bread and soup. Tastes like crap."

"You were expecting fine dining?" Lacey asked.

"He must put something in it," Victoria said. "Every time I eat, I throw up."

"Sounds like he's treating the food, giving you barely enough to keep you alive. Which is weakening your body and immune system. He could be lacing the soup with an emetic. That would account for the vomiting. Your electrolytes are probably shot."

"Are you a doctor?" Melinda asked.

Lacey shook her head. "I was pre-med at NYU. First day in the cadaver lab I realized I couldn't handle it. Apparently, surgery wasn't my calling. I switched over to philosophy and English literature instead."

"That's odd," Melinda said.

"What? That I'd choose history and the classics over the limelight of a surgical suite?"

"No. That we'd both be history and literature majors. I'm doing my PhD at Harvard. Ancient Mythology. You?"

"I'm working towards a degree in psychology," Lacey replied. "But the old tales have always fascinated me."

"There's something very familiar about you," Melinda said. "Did you attend Harvard?"

"No," Lacey answered. "But I recently attended a Harvard sponsored seminar."

"Where?"

"NYU." Lacey looked confused. "Why?"

"Dr. Jane Belay's lecture by any chance?"

"Yes," Lacey said. "On Folklore and Mythology. She was

speaking at a rare book shop. Kessel's Bookbinding and Restoration."

"I was at that seminar," Melinda said. "That's how I know you. I saw you there." Melinda paused. "The odds that the two of us would have attended the same seminar and wind up here are next to impossible. He targeted us," Melinda said.

Lacey nodded. "But why?"

"Did you say Kessel's?" Victoria asked. "I sell rare paper. Mrs. Kessel was one of my biggest customers."

Across the room, tending to her wounds, Bonnie joined the conversation. "My family's company is the largest provider of aged and period leather in the country. Book restoration companies are some of our oldest clients. Anyone but me seeing a connection here?"

"Yeah," Lacey said. "Books, paper, leather, book repair. This guy is in the industry."

"But why take us?" Melinda asked. "Lacey and I are just students."

"Maybe for that precise reason," Bonnie offered. "Perhaps folklore and mythology are his main areas of interest. He sees you as his peers. Your expert knowledge would make you ideal prisoners… and conversationalists."

"Like that will ever happen," Lacey said. "I'm not about to talk shop with that freak."

"Our ability to do that might be the only thing that will stop him from killing us," Bonnie said.

Victoria agreed. "He has an unusually strong connection to you, Lacey," she said. "He said he wants you to be his wife. Which means we are expendable. We already know he's not altogether there, probably even insane. Be careful what you say to him. Frankly, our lives are in your hands."

"I don't want that responsibility," Lacey said. "I'm the one who dropped out of medical school, remember?"

"Whether you want it or not isn't the issue," Victoria replied. "You've got it. It's yours."

"Not if I can get us out of here," Lacey replied.

# 12

OTTO SCHREIBER FELL forward as the bullet tore through his backpack, passed through his shoulder, then pinged off the steel entrance door to Lacey's apartment. Stupid, he thought. Why had he not checked the man for a weapon when he was down?

The gun wavered in Anton's hand. He tried pushing his body up off the floor, fell back. The blow to the back of his head had been severe and affected his balance. Vertigo had set in. The room was spinning. He dropped the gun, picked it up again, forced himself to fight the rising darkness and the overwhelming desire to pass out, raised the weapon and fired wildly. Adrenaline trumped accuracy. He could process the sound of the gunshots in his mind but not the trajectory of the rounds. Anton emptied the clip, exhausted the weapon. Darkness now gave way to light, psychological impairment to mental acuity. Having regained his senses, he suddenly realized he had been firing the weapon in the opposite direction of the doorway; he had been shooting *into* the apartment. He reeled around, searched for his attacker.

The door was open.

The man with the backpack was gone.

Anton rose to one knee, struggled to both feet, then shuffled down the hall toward the front entrance of the apartment.

The presence of the intruder, coupled with the assault, meant one thing. His instinct was right. Lacey was in danger.

Anton pushed open the door, grabbed the handrail for support. Outside, the bright sunlight stung his eyes. The pain at the point of impact where he had been struck flared. He touched the area, expected blood, found none. God, it hurt.

He scanned the street, saw no sign of his attacker. In the distance, the wail of sirens. Across the street, a woman screamed. Two pedestrians walking their dogs in the quiet enclave ran for cover, one behind a parked car, the other the corner of an adjoining building. The women were staring at him, cellphones in hand, talking quickly. Initially, the reason for their harried behavior and overt concern didn't compute with Anton. Then he felt the weight of the gun in his hand.

The sirens were drawing closer. Were they on their way to Lacey's apartment? Had *he* been the subject of the phone calls? Had someone called 9-1-1?

Anton shoved the gun into his waistband and slowly made his way to his car. The passersby had surely taken down his license plate number and called it into the authorities already. He would need to get off the street as soon as possible. One street over, a twenty-four-hour long-term parking garage offered an escape.

Speeding up the circular ramp, he found an available parking spot on the seventh level and quickly backed in his car. The authorities would eventually find the vehicle during their sweep of the area; that much was certain. But for the time being out of sight was out of mind, and out of sight also meant more time for him to continue his search for his assailant. He wouldn't be hard to find. Though the morning was slightly cooler than it had been for the past week, the man was overdressed for the weather, wearing jeans, a dark blue hoodie, running shoes and leather driving gloves. Whether he had been driving or fled on foot was unknown. By the time Anton had recovered and pursued his attacker the man was long gone. He was sure he had gotten off at least one clean round before falling semi-conscious. He had noticed a tiny dent in the door at approximately the same height as the man and a chip of paint missing on its otherwise perfectly maintained surface. Perhaps one of the rounds had struck him.

Anton removed his cellphone and made a call.

"Odyssey Gentleman's Club."

"Cindy, it's Anton."

"Anton, where the hell are you?" Cindy Simms was personal secretary to the Odyssey's owner, Russ Paley. "Russ has been asking for you. He's thoroughly pissed that you're not here."

"I'm heading back to the club now. Is Mike around?"

"The limo driver? Yeah. Why?"

"I need a lift back to the club. Car trouble," he lied. "Wallet's locked in the car along with my credit cards and cash."

Cindy snickered. "That was brilliant."

"*Mike?*"

"Hang on."

Mike Degario picked up the line a few seconds later. "I hear you're in need of my services," he teased. "You know I charge double for personal pickups."

Anton agreed. "Sorry, Mike. It was a bonehead play on my part. Think you can swing into Brooklyn and pick me up?"

"Sure. Where are you?"

"Parking garage. About a block from Lacey Chastain's place."

"You dog."

"It's not like that. I came by to check on her. No one's seen her. She's not here. I think she may be in..."

Anton stopped talking. From his seventh-floor vantage point behind the railing of the car park he saw his attacker in the distance.

Four streets over, the hooded man, backpack slung over his shoulder, stopped beside a silver Bentley parked on the street. Anton watched him open the door, throw the bag in the backseat, and climb into the car slowly, one hand applying pressure to his shoulder. He appeared to be injured.

"Anton?" Degario said.

Anton didn't respond. He focused on the man, straining to get a better look at him, couldn't.

"You still there?"

Anton answered. "Cancel the pickup, Mikey. I gotta go."

"You sure?" Degario said. "I can be there in..."

Anton ended the call, ran to the stairwell at the end of the parking garage, threw open the door, and bounded down the steps two at a time.

If he ran fast enough, he could catch up to the Bentley, pull the man out of his car and throttle him within an inch of his life to find out what he knew about Lacey's disappearance.

His head ached.

His body ached.
His heart ached.
He ran faster.

## 13

AGENT PENNER STARED at the blood-soaked concrete cutting saw standing in the middle of the plastic sheeted room.

"How in God's name did you know this was here?" he asked.

Jordan stared at the ghost standing in the corner of the room then watched her image fade. The dead had a way of communicating that was unique unto them. It satisfied Courtney Valentine that Jordan would do what needed to be done to make her story known and turn up the heat in the search for her killer. Jordan acknowledged the specter with a nod, then turned her attention back to the crime scene.

Chris leaned over and examined the machine. "Fragments of flesh and bone," he said. "All over the blade and into the assembly of the saw itself. Jesus, he made one hell of a mess. Hard to believe no one heard her. There were no cries for help, no 9-1-1 calls from neighboring residents... nothing."

"She was drugged," Jordan said. "Whatever he gave her

was strong enough to incapacitate her. She wouldn't have been able to do a damn thing to stop it."

"What kind of person does this to another human being?" Penner said angrily.

"The kind who is egotistical enough to taunt the cops with handwritten notes and thinks we'll never catch him."

"To that, I'd say his batting average has been damn good so far," Penner replied. "He's making the NYPD look like rank amateurs. No wonder Haley wants this guy's head on a stick."

Jordan walked around the room, getting a feel for the scene. Courtney Valentine would return on her own time if she ever did. Jordan acutely knew the responsibility the dead woman had imparted to her. Her communications with the deceased were solemn and sacred. They talked to her in their own mysterious way and she listened. In the corner of the room, she found an item of interest: a length of frayed red ribbon.

"You said Scroll always leaves a calling card, right? A handwritten note?" Jordan asked.

Penner nodded. "At every scene."

"Did they find one with the remains? In one of the plastic garbage bags?"

The agent hesitated. "Come to think of it, no. We identified her by reaching out to the hospital. Her scrubs were soaked in blood and shredded as you saw. But our guys identified ink on the fabric under the blood. We could piece together enough sections of the garment to make out her first initial, a period, and the first few letters of her last name. The hospital logo was silk-screened inside the collar of the top she was wearing. We confirmed the scrubs were theirs. Staff records showed no other employees had that combination of letters in their last and first name. We concluded it had to be Courtney."

"Why wouldn't he leave a note?" Chris said. "I mean, let's face it. The guy's ego wouldn't permit him to let her death go without receiving credit for the kill."

"Chris is right," Penner agreed. "A guy like this needs that acknowledgement. It's an adrenaline rush for him. There's no way he wouldn't take credit for her death."

"He did," Jordan said, sifting through a plastic pail full of construction scraps. She removed small sections of broken drywall, pieces of concrete, nails, and miscellaneous debris. "He wanted us to work for it." She held up a piece of leather-like material, rolled tightly and tied with a red ribbon.

"You found a scroll?" Chris said. He and Penner walked toward Jordan as she examined the note in the dim light of the room.

Jordan nodded. "Got a flashlight?" she asked.

Penner removed a penlight from his jacket pocket. "Will this do?"

"Perfect," Jordan said. She untied the ribbon and unraveled the note.

"The material looks different," Penner said.

"That's because it's dried human flesh," Jordan said. "He's escalated. He's way past homemade parchment now. He's using their skin as a writing pad."

The section of skin measured approximately four inches by six inches. Jordan read the note aloud. "Dear Commissioner Haley. You think your streets are safe. They're not. You think your citizens are safe. They're not. I took my time with this one. Sorry about the mess. I can assure you a good time was had by all. Tell your task force I said hello."

"Condescending bastard," Penner said.

"He can be as condescending as he wants," Chris

replied. "The ball's in his court and he just served up another ace."

Touching the skin-scroll, Jordan felt the familiar head pain that came with the sudden rush of an intense psychic connection. She saw the woman on the table in the makeshift surgical suite, watched as her tormentor excised the section of skin from her body that would become the note, heard the screams, then realized the pleas for help were not coming from the woman to whom the skin belonged but to others in the room with her.

The connection was too intense. Jordan broke it and handed Chris the scroll. "This woman is not alone. He's keeping others."

"Keeping?" Chris asked.

"He has prisoners. Many of them." Jordan felt the attacker's energy on the scroll. "He plans to kill them."

"Can you see where they are?" Penner asked.

Jordan closed her eyes, tried hard to reconnect with the skin donor's surroundings, saw nothing.

"I'm sorry," she said. "That's all I'm getting right now."

"Don't worry, Jordan," Chris said. "It'll come to you. It always does."

"For the sake of the victims it better come fast," Penner said. The agent's cellphone rang. He walked away and took the call.

"That guy is in serious need of an attitude adjustment," Chris said to his partner.

"He's just upset," Jordan replied. "We all are."

"You can't work the case any faster than your ability will permit."

"It's nothing," Jordan said. "Everyone's on edge right now. All the way up to the Mayor's office."

Agent Penner returned. "That was Keon. Somebody just

called in a missing person's report. He thinks it might be a good idea if we meet with her in person. Woman's name is Shona-Lee Cairns."

"Sounds good," Chris said. "Where to now?"

"Manhattan. Odyssey Gentlemen's Club. Cairns believes one of their dancers is missing. A woman by the name of Lacey Chastain."

Chris took out his phone. "I'll call forensics, get them over here."

Penner surveyed the blood-spattered room. "Better tell them to send two teams. Looks like they're gonna be here for a while."

# 14

OTTO SCHREIBER OPENED the door to his silver Bentley and fell into the driver's seat. The pain from the bullet wound in his shoulder was made worse by his walk to the car. The gunfire had caught him completely off guard. The man he attacked in Lacey Chastain's apartment had been down, possibly dead. He had struck a violent blow to the back of his head, heard the sickening crack of the bat as it made contact. The blow should have killed him or at the very least rendered him unconscious for the next few hours.

He sat in the seat, trying to control his labored breathing, massaging the area of penetration, evaluating the severity of the shoulder wound. The sound of the gunfire had created a post-traumatic onslaught of horrific memories of his time spent in captivity. His skin crawled. He wanted to scream. His condition, allodynia, was raging havoc on his body, physically and mentally. He grabbed hold of the steering wheel and squeezed hard, trying to control the symptoms, to displace their effect and quell the intensity of the attack. Eventually it would subside. Until then all he could do was hold on and ride the wave of pain like a surfer caught in a crashing wave, ride the rip and roll with it, unsure of what condition his body would be in when eventually he found the surface, or the undertow claimed him. The hundreds of tiny scars on his skin perpetrated by the barbed bamboo body wrap came alive, as though they were not part of his skin at all but rather an interconnected mass of malignant cells which covered his body, each refusing to surrender to apoptosis and die. Instead, they fed on his neuralgic state, pulsing, throbbing, and burning like thousands of smoldering cinders in a fire stoked deep beneath his skin. His condition seemed to be getting worse, not better, failing to improve with the drug therapy his doctors at Bellevue had assured him would dramatically reduce his pain. The sensation suggested thoughts of what it must feel like to be burned alive. The irony of the moment was not lost on him. The effects of his enormously painful condition would make a tremendous addition to his knowledge of torture if only he could learn how to replicate it.

He forced himself to move. He turned on the car, pushed the START button, and put the vehicle in gear. Several streets away he heard the sound of approaching sirens, no doubt en route to Lacey's apartment. The police were likely responding to the report of gunshots. On arrival, they would find the man on the floor of the apartment. After receiving medical attention, he would explain his reason for discharging the weapon. Otto doubted the man had had any opportunity to see him, much less be able to identify him. He had come at him too fast, attacked him from behind before he had had the chance to turn and defend himself. He should have finished him off, split his head open with the bat. Who was he to Lacey, anyway? Surely not her boyfriend. Otto had been watching her for the past few weeks, observing her routine. He knew where she shopped, what time she left for school or the club and could recognize any of her girlfriends who visited her regularly. A trained observer, he had kept detailed notes. Lacey's private life seemed to revolve around the Odyssey, traveling to and from NYU and her tabby cat, Prince Harry. He had observed her in the grocery store from the end of the aisle, watched as she stocked up on Fancy Feast, Harry's preferred cuisine. She had almost caught him looking at her. He had avoided eye contact by raising his hand and rubbing his temple, shielding his face from view. Not wanting to be seen watching her, he left the store and followed her home. The hour had been late, the streets empty. He debated whether to abduct her. He was prepared. In his pocket, he carried a small aerosol canister which contained his special formula of equal parts sevoflurane, isoflurane, ether, halothane, and Fentanyl. On contact with air the potent blend of liquids created a gas which when inhaled immediately induced a state of deep sleep. It had taken him many attempts to get the combination of ingredients just right. Earlier test subjects had died inhaling the deadly mixture, their airway seizing immediately, breathing stopped. He had considered keeping their bodies in the bookstore dungeon as trophies but preferred the company of the living to the dead. Instead, he disposed of them at various locations around the city, leaving each with a note; the first in the trunk of an abandoned car on a side street in Bedford-Stuyvesant, the second in an alley frequented by drug-addled vagrants in Queens, the third in a drainage culvert on the bank of the Hudson River. Following the news and listening to the reports made by Commissioner Haley about the progress his department was making on the killings had been entertaining. In fact, they did not have a clue who or what they were dealing with. It was then Otto decided it would be amusing to direct all the notes to Haley himself. The media soon put the pompous police leader in his place, publicly chastising him for misleading them and taking advantage of the public trust. This pleased Otto to no end.

He had to get back to the book repair shop. Lacey would be waiting for him, probably even worried about him, as any devout wife-to-be would be. She would need the finery he had picked out for her. He would let her out of the strappado tonight, perhaps even permit her to take a good long soak in a hot bath and make her a nice meal. After dinner, before relaxing for the evening, he would excuse himself. The woman on the hospital gurney would probably be dead by now. He would need to dispose of the body.

As Otto pulled away from the curb a tremendous *thud* struck the back of the Bentley. He looked in his side-view mirror and saw the man from Lacey's apartment rushing the driver's door, gun in hand.

Otto hit the gas. The Bentley responded, tires screaming. The smell of burning rubber wafted up from the pavement.

The first bullet shattered the back window.

The second blew out his side mirror.

Otto dropped low in his seat and stayed out of the line of fire as the next three rounds ripped into the back of the luxury automobile.

The car careened around the corner, leaving the gunman behind.

Otto slammed the steering wheel with his fist. *Why the hell didn't I kill the sonofabitch when I had the chance?*

. . .

STANDING ON THE STREET, gun in hand, sirens approaching, Anton Moore repeated the license plate number of the Bentley aloud: "ABN 2431... ABN 2431... ABN 2431..."

Then he ran.

# 15

LACEY SEARCHED THE dungeon for a secondary exit, found none. The door at the top of the stairs was locked. She kicked it. "Damn it!" she yelled.

"It's no use, Lacey," Melinda said. "The only way in and out of here is through that door. And we hear him lock it every time he leaves."

"Maybe we should wait until he comes back," Bonnie said. "Then surprise him."

"How do you propose we do that?" Lacey asked. "You can barely walk, and Melinda and Victoria are locked in their cells."

"Then you need to get us out of here," Melinda said. "Between the three of us we could take him. He's weak, I can tell. He moves slowly, like he's in pain. He wouldn't be a match for us. Try the cells doors again."

"They're bolted into the floor and it's solid concrete," Victoria said. "They won't budge."

"But the ceiling isn't," Melinda said. "It's made of wood, old wood. Look." She pointed to several planks into which the metal top rail of her cell was affixed using heavy screws.

"If we can work those loose, we might be able to pull the cell wall free from the ceiling. Even if the gap is small, I might be able to squeeze through. I'm small. I could do it."

"Check the closet where he keeps the medical supplies," Victoria suggested. "He used tools to build this place. Maybe he still keeps a few around."

Lacey walked to the closet, opened the door, rummaged around. She removed a small metal box hidden behind cardboard boxes of medical supplies and rummaged through its contents. The box contained a hammer, two screwdrivers, four wood chisels, two containers of aluminum solder paste, a can of penetrating oil, a miniature butane torch, matches, a hacksaw and an assortment of metal filing rasps. "Bingo," Lacey said. She held up a hammer and chisel, showed them to Melinda. "Think you can reach the ceiling?"

"I can try. Why?"

"Use these to break the screws," Lacey asked. "Jam the chisel under the top rail where it meets the ceiling. Slam it with the hammer. Give it everything you've got. With luck, you'll snap the screw. Break them all and the top of the cell wall should give way."

"I can try," Melinda said. Lacey handed her the tools. Melinda stood on the tips of her toes. Even with her arms fully extended the ceiling was still out of reach. "I can't do it. I'm not tall enough."

"Then we'll make you taller," Lacey said. She looked around the room. "I have an idea."

Lacey brought the metal toolbox over to Melinda's cell and pushed it through the bars. "Try standing on that," she asked.

Melinda kicked the box into position and stood on it, testing its ability to hold her weight. The old box, made from heavy steel, provided exactly the extra height she needed to reach the ceiling.

"Got it," Melinda said.

"Whenever you're ready," Lacey said, "hit that screw as hard as you can."

Bonnie and Victoria watched as Melinda found the location of the screw hole, positioned the chisel in front, then found her balance on the toolbox. "Here goes," Melinda said.

She slammed the end of the chisel handle with the hammer. The tool cut cleanly through the screw and jutted out on the other side of the cell wall at the ceiling.

"It worked!" Melinda yelled. She wrenched the chisel free of the top rail.

"Good," Lacey said. "Keep working the rest of the screws the same way, then pass the box and tools through to Victoria. Vicky, break the screws loose from your side. Then we'll bring it down."

"Will do," Victoria replied.

Melinda slid the toolbox along the floor from one screw location to the next. Within a few minutes she had severed all the ceiling screws in her cell and passed the box and implements to Victoria.

"Your turn, Vicky," Lacey said. Victoria followed Melinda's lead and broke through each of the heavy screws which secured the top rail of her cell to the wooden ceiling.

"Done," she said.

"All right," Lacey said. "Moment of truth. You ready?"

"Ready," the women replied.

"On three, push," Lacey instructed. "One... two... three!"

Weak of energy but mighty with a desire to be free from captivity, Melinda and Victoria pushed hard against the cage's steel bars. The cell wall swayed. It bent forward a few inches from the top rail. The bottom rail, anchored to the concrete floor with heavy duty bolts, refused to budge.

Victoria sat on the floor of her cell. “It’s not enough,” she said. “It won’t come down.” She was on the verge of tears.

“It’s coming down one way or the other,” Lacey said. “Bonnie, are you strong enough to help me?”

“I’ll do whatever you need me to do,” Bonnie replied.

“All right. We’re going to pull this thing down,” Lacey said. She untied the rope from the strappado and secured it to the fatigued top rail.

“Here’s the plan,” Lacey said. “Both of you lean against the cell bars at the same time as we pull down on the rope. When you have enough room, shimmy through the gap and get out.”

“Got it,” Melinda said.

Victoria remained seated on the floor, refused to move. “You’re wasting your time,” she said. “It’s no use. We’re never getting out of here.”

Lacey walked over to her. “Stand up, Vicky,” she said.

Vicky looked up at her, eyes glistening, said nothing, didn’t move.

Lacey knelt. “Come over here,” she said.

Vicky dropped her head.

“Come on. Scoot over here. Right now.”

Slowly, Victoria slid over. Lacey took her hand through the bars. “Now, repeat after me: ‘He’ll never hurt me again.’”

Victoria shook her head. Her voice quivered. “But he will.”

“No, he won’t,” Lacey said firmly. “You know how close you are right now to being free of him and this place? Twelve inches. One measly foot. Because that’s how far down Bonnie and I will pull these damn bars. Then you and

Melinda will crawl through the top gap and slip out on this side. And you know what happens then?"

"We get out of here?"

"Exactly."

"But the door is locked."

"Leave that to me," Lacey said. "The first thing Bonnie and I need is for you two to get out of those cells. Now, you ready?"

"I think so."

"I know so," Lacey said confidently. "C'mon on, baby. Up on your feet."

As instructed, the two women positioned themselves against the bars of their cell.

"Ready?" Lacey asked.

"Ready," the women replied.

"Now!" Lacey pulled down as hard as she could on the rope as Melinda and Victoria pushed against the bars. The cell wall slowly gave way. Fatigued and weakened, it leaned forward by several more inches, then fell forward.

Lacey and Bonnie waited until both women had freed themselves from their cells and fell over the top rail to the ground at their feet. Elated at their escape, physically spent, emotionally drained, Melinda and Victoria wept. Lacey and Bonnie held them in their arms, comforted them.

Bonnie turned to Lacey. "Now what?" She pointed to the door at the top of the stairs. "We're still locked in here."

Lacey smiled. "Piece of cake."

"What are you planning to do?"

"Blow the door."

## 16

ANTON RAN AFTER the silver car, aimed his gun at the vehicle, ready to fire again at the fleeing Bentley, then watched as it disappeared around the corner. He lowered the weapon and shoved it in his pocket. A cacophony of sirens echoed off the walls of the surrounding low-rises, apartment buildings and retail shops. The 9-1-1 response had been swift and immediate. A fire truck and ambulance sped past followed by two NYPD squad cars. Down the street, a city bus was approaching. Anton jogged across the road, waited for the transit vehicle to stop, hopped on, took a seat, and called Mike Degario.

"Mike, me again."

"Nice of you to hang up on me, buddy," Degario said.

"Sorry," Anton replied. "I wasn't in much of a position to talk. I need a favor."

"You always need a favor. Five minutes ago, that favor was picking you up in Brooklyn. What is it now? Bailing your ass out of jail?"

"Nothing like that. That P.I. you know, Ray Jensen. You two still in touch?"

"Yeah. He owes me nearly as many favors as you do. Why?"

"I need him to run a plate for me."

"That's something only the cops can do."

"Come on, Mikey. You and I both know that's bullshit. There isn't a self-respecting private investigator on the planet that doesn't have the police contacts to run a license plate. And I wouldn't ask if it wasn't important."

"This about Lacey?"

"Yeah."

"Anton, what the hell is going on? Let me help you."

Anton felt the lump on the back of his head. "Forget it, Mike. It's too dangerous. Just do me that favor. Tell him it's a matter of life and death. Write this down: ABN 2431. Belongs to a silver Bentley sedan. I think it's the same car that picked up Lacey from the club last night. It's got to be. I need that plate. It could be my only connection to finding her. I don't have time to waste, Mike. Can you help me or not?

Degario sighed. "Jesus, you should have been in sales, not security. All right, all right. I'll make the call. I can't give you any guarantees Jensen will come through, but at least I can say I tried. You good with that?"

"Absolutely. Couldn't ask for more."

"Yeah, you could. And knowing you, before the day's out, you probably will."

"Thanks, Mikey. I owe you one."

"No, you owe me a *dozen*."

"I stand corrected."

"All right. Wait for my call. I'll get back to you as soon as I can. Where are you now?"

"On a bus."

"A bus?"

"It's a long story."

"Sounds like one."

"Maybe I'll take you up on your offer."

"To pick you up?"

"Yeah."

"You still in Brooklyn?"

"Yeah."

"Whereabouts?"

Anton stared out the window. The bus slowed as it passed Nostrand Avenue. The street was cordoned off as police interviewed the residents standing outside Lacey's building. The brakes shuddered. The bus jerked ahead and resumed its route. Anton looked out the window. "Flushing Avenue," he said. "Coming up on Graham."

"I know it," Degario said. "You'll hit Woodhull Hospital in a couple of stops. Get off. I'll meet you there. Give me an hour."

"Thanks, Mike."

"You got it."

## 17

JORDAN, CHRIS AND Agent Max Penner presented their credentials to the doorman at the Odyssey Gentlemen's Club. The man spoke into the walkie-talkie microphone clipped to his shirt collar and directed them inside. Shona Lee-Cairns met them at the bar. "Follow me upstairs to the VIP lounge," she said. "It's sound-proofed and at this time of the morning it's empty. We still have a couple of hours before the lunch crowd rolls in."

The pounding rock music accompanying the current dancer's performance on the main floor was inaudible in the VIP lounge. The music too was different; upscale; sexy, the sultry sound of jazz, intended to create a relaxed environment for the club's more affluent patrons and highest tippers.

Shona looked at Chris. "Have we met before?" she asked.

"No ma'am," Chris replied. "Can't say as I've had the pleasure."

"You look familiar to me. Have you been here before?"

"I'm afraid not."

"Too bad. You should stop by sometime. I'll arrange a private dance for you if you like."

Penner and Jordan glanced at Chris. The agent blushed. "Thank you, ma'am. But the bureau has rules."

"Rules, shmooles," Shona said. She winked. "Tell you what. You play by your rules, I'll play by mine."

Although he was enjoying listening to the inherent sexual innuendo being directed at his colleague, Agent Penner saved Chris from further embarrassment. "Ms. Cairns," he began. "It's our understanding you believe one of your colleagues is missing?"

Shona nodded. "That's right. Lacey Chastain. She's a featured dancer here at the club."

"When did you last speak with her?"

"Last night."

Penner leaned forward in his chair. "Last night?" he repeated. "Ma'am, with all due respect, why did you call the police to report your friend missing? It's been less than twelve hours."

"Because I know something is wrong. I feel it."

Penner stood. He returned the notepad and pen to his pocket. "I'm sorry, Ms. Cairns. We can't help you. I can arrange for a uniformed officer to drop by Ms. Chastain's place and do a wellness check if you like. Other than that..."

Jordan interrupted. "You said Ms. Chastain is a featured dancer here at the club?"

"Yes, that's right."

"Then she has a private dressing room."

"Yes."

"May I see it?"

"Of course," Shona said. She seemed puzzled by the request. "It's downstairs. Come with me."

The change room was small but brightly decorated. It

was comprised of Lacey's make-up desk and chair, both of which were upholstered in faux-leopard skin. The room smelled of lavender and expensive perfume. Signed head shots and promotional pictures of actors and professional athletes covered the walls. A collection of stuffed animals, gifts from fans according to Shona, sat in a guest chair in the corner. Lacey's personal locker stood beside the chair. The padlock hung open, unlocked.

"That's weird," Shona said. "Lacey's very particular about her privacy. It's not like her to leave her locker open like that."

Jordan opened the metal door. Among Lacey's belongings were a pair of jeans and sneakers, street clothes, three satin nightclub dresses, two pairs of high heels, a riding crop, several pairs of lace body stockings, massage oil, a bottle of Chanel perfume, makeup, and an open envelope. Jordan touched the envelope and received a flood of images: the invitation it had contained; the pretty blonde herself; the two-thousand dollars in cash someone had paid her to attend the affair, and the dark energy of the man they had dubbed the Scroll Killer. The ornate handwriting on the envelope, written in calligraphy, read *Ms. Lacey Chastain–Private and Confidential.*

"That's why I called you," Shona-Lee said. "Lacey received that invitation two days ago asking her to attend a private function."

"Meaning she's a pro," Agent Penner said.

"Only part-time," Shona-Lee said.

Jordan turned to Chris and handed him the envelope. "It's him," she said. "It's Scroll."

"You sure?"

"I'm certain," Jordan said. "Check out the handwriting, the stylization." From her purse she removed the scroll she recovered from the construction site and showed it to the two agents. "It's a match."

"Are you saying this complaint is legit?" Penner asked. "Scroll has this woman?"

"I am."

Penner's questions came fast and furious. "Is she alive? Where can we find her? What about the others?"

Jordan took back the envelope from her partner, closed her eyes and concentrated. She saw Lacey going about her day, attending class at NYU, the delivery of the envelope to the bartender at the Odyssey.

She addressed Shona-Lee. "The envelope was hand-delivered, right?"

"That's correct."

"But not by courier."

"No."

"You know this person. Or at least they're known to the club."

"Yes. Father Frank dropped it off."

"A priest dropped off the envelope?" Penner asked.

Shona-Lee shook her head. "Father Frank Who Lives Under the Bridge.' At least that's what we call him."

"That's one you're going to have to explain," Penner said.

"Father Frank is homeless. He lives under the overpass around the corner. He's a veteran. Used to be a military chaplain overseas until he lost an eye in Iraq. That wasn't all he lost either. He lost himself over there, too. Russ, the Odyssey's owner, is his brother. He's tried to help him get off the street countless times, but Father Frank is happy right where he is. Russ lets him stay downstairs when it gets too cold or the weather gets terrible outside, feeds him and Biscuit, cleans him up, that sort of thing."

"Biscuit?" Chris asked.

"Frank's dog. The most beautiful German Shepherd you've ever seen. Biscuit's an absolute baby but crazy protective of Frank. Get too close without Frank's permission and Biscuit will have your hand down his throat before you know what happened. Trust me, anyone who knows what's good for them knows better than to mess with Frank and Biscuit."

"And you said Frank lives nearby?"

"Yes. Under the overpass."

"How will we find him?"

"He tagged the entrance to his place. You can't miss it."

"What does it say?" Chris asked.

"Semper Fi, followed by the sign of the Cross."

# 18

OTTO SCHREIBER KNEW driving the bullet-riddled Bentley with the blown out back window and shattered side mirror for much longer would be impossible. One thing for which New York could be counted on was a significant police presence. One glance at the vehicle by a passing cop and he would be pulled over. The damaged car would be deemed unsafe to drive in its present condition. Questions would follow: how did the vehicle come to receive the bullet holes? Had he reported the incident to police? The unsatisfactory answers he would provide the authorities would immediately raise suspicion about him and lead to unwanted scrutiny. The last thing he wanted was give the police any reason to look closely at him over what amounted to little more than motor vehicle infractions.

Two blocks down the road, a convenience store parking lot offered the solution he was looking for. He backed the Bentley into a spot between a rusted Cadillac, sitting on concrete blocks, and a grocery store delivery van, the sides of which had been freshly tagged with gang symbols. The vandalized vehicle bore four flat tires, a broken windshield and smashed out brake lights; evidence perhaps that the proprietor had refused to pay protection money to the thugs to leave his small business and family alone. In this part of town, you either cooperated with the gangs or you paid the price. Otto wondered just how tough the gang members really were. Perhaps he would abduct one of them for fun, strap him to the hospital gurney in his dungeon, and remove his skin layer by layer. Naturally, he would have to forego the use of an anesthetic. After all, this would be an exercise to learn just how much pain the street punk could tolerate. Otto's guess was that he wouldn't last thirty seconds before he would start screaming for his mommy. How pathetic, he thought. Tough guy, my ass.

Having abandoned the car, Otto walked to the street corner and hailed a cab. The pain in his shoulder was incredible. When he got back to the bookstore Lacey would tend to his injury. Although he had never felt it, he knew her touch would be gentle. She would clean and dress the wound, perhaps even apply a few stitches if needed. He knew she would be attentive to his needs.

He began his search for a wife three years ago. What was her name? Annie?... Amy?... Angie? It had been so long ago he had nearly forgotten. *Amy*. Yes, that was it. She had been a stewardess, on layover from Chicago, in town for the evening. They met at the Acola nightclub, in Miami. The city had been his home for six months. He enjoyed the hustle and bustle, wealth, beautiful women, and neon-clad night life it offered. Before that he had lived in Atlanta, Raleigh, Nashville, Washington, and Pittsburgh. He liked being on the move. Travel provided him with freedom. His time spent in captivity had taught him a valuable lesson: life was precious and to be lived without compromise. He had given up enough of his life in service to his country. Now it was time to live it on his terms, settle down and get married. But the latter had proven to be much more of a challenge than he had expected. The hundreds of scars, hidden from view by his clothing, were hideous. Coupled with his medical condition, he was barely able to handle the sensation of his clothing against his body, much less the intimate touch of another human being. Otto knew it was a matter of time before he found the right woman to share his life with. But constant denial had left him humiliated, embarrassed and emotionally broken. Why had Amy found it necessary to make him feel less of a man? He could have treasured her, made her the center of his world. But no, she had to laugh, to jeer, ridicule him, bring him down. The mental anguish of it all had been too much to bear. Before slitting her throat, she had called him a monster. In that moment he had thought of Mary Shelley's classic tale of horror, Frankenstein, and how he had been created; tortured, disfigured, experimented upon, and transformed. If this was to be his life, one of solitude and shame, loneliness, and despair, then he would do everything in his power to exert what little control he had left over it. There had to be someone out there for him. He would simply have to sort through them, disposing of all who served no viable purpose. He re-experienced the event for days: the cutting of her throat, the wave of anger that had washed over him, the image of her gaping neck, the vacant look on her face, and asked himself the same question: *Why*. Why did he have to kill her? Why in taking her life had he seen not her face but the face of his captor? Why, in his mind, had he not been in his apartment but rather in his cell in Iraq? Why, after murdering her, did he find it necessary to lock her body in his bathroom, then barricade himself in his bedroom? Days later, when he had regained his mental balance, he put the thoughts of the event out of his mind and rationalized the situation. Lack of sleep and time to think had left him psychologically and emotionally inoculated. Her death was not his fault. He was not to blame. She made him do it. She had brought the end of her life upon herself. She had been responsible for his withdrawal from the world. He cut up the body and disposed of its parts in various locations around the city. He expected to be caught and fully expected the police would break down his door and take him into custody at any moment. But that day never came. They never sought him out. Fear soon gave way to confidence, confidence to cockiness. Now, New York City had become his killing ground. Murder had become a game, one at which he was extremely adept at playing.

Otto opened the door and eased himself into the back seat of the cab.

"Where to?" the driver asked.

"Manhattan," Otto replied.

"You sure?"

"Why wouldn't I be?"

"A trip that far is gonna cost you a small fortune."

"I'm good for it."

The cabbie smiled. "Works for me. It'll take us a few minutes to get out of here though. Tons of cops around. Something's going down."

Otto thought of Lacey... the sweetness of her voice, the perfection of her body, how she was the one for whom he had been searching for so long.

"You okay, man?" the cabbie asked.

It was then Otto realized he had fallen. He lay slumped against the door. He straightened up, looked ahead.

"Fine," he replied. "Just drive."

## 19

ON THE RETURN trip from Brooklyn to Manhattan, Mike Degario took the private investigator's call. "Thanks, Ray. I appreciate your help," he said. He glanced at Anton. "That was my buddy. He called in a marker at NYPD and got you the info on the Bentley. Plate comes back to a guy by the name of Otto Schreiber."

"Where do I find him?"

"What do you mean, *you*? We're a team now, buddy. It's obvious this guy's too dangerous for you to track down on your own. Which means you inherited a new partner. Namely, me."

"I can't let you do that, Mikey. You'll get hurt."

"You have no choice in the matter. I'm in. So's Russ. He called earlier. I brought him up to speed on the situation. Had to. He was ready to fire your ass for leaving the club without notice. He's assembling a team to help find Lacey. You know how heavily connected he is. He ordered me to drive you back to the Odyssey to tell him everything you know about what's happened to Lacey. We'll track her down together. Everyone in the club loves that girl, not just you."

"Thanks, Mike."

"We're gonna get her back, Anton. I promise."

Anton stared out the passenger window of the limousine. Block by block, the city flashed by. He offered no reply.

"One more thing," Mike said.

"What's that?"

"Russ said to tell you he'll see that whoever took Lacey is properly dealt with. Sonofabitch is gonna regret the day he was born."

"She's in deep trouble, Mike. I can feel it. You know the club rules: unless it's you driving her home, no dancer catches a ride until I've checked the driver's ID before she gets in the car. I messed up big time."

"It was Lacey," Degario reminded him. "You never think straight when she's around."

"She'll never forgive me for letting this happen to her."

"All right, big man," Mike said. "That shit ends now. Lacey's a big girl. And this pick up was off the books. She's had bad dates in the past. There was nothing you could have done about those either."

"I know."

"The guy one-upped you. Deal with it. Move on and never let it happen again. You're gonna have a small army on your side soon. You should have heard the anger in Russ' voice. When we find this guy, he's as good as dead. And if we're going to do that, you need to have your head in the game. Got it?"

Anton nodded. "Yeah, I got it."

"Good. Now tell me what you know about him so far."

"Not much. Five-foot ten, maybe one-eighty. Blue

hoodie, jeans, and a backpack. I got off a round. I'm pretty sure it caught him in the shoulder."

"You shot him?"

"I shot *at* him. He hit me damn hard. With a baseball bat, I think."

"You're lucky he didn't kill you."

"He should have."

"Age?"

"Don't know. His back was turned to me. I only caught a glimpse of his face. If I had to guess I'd say mid-thirties."

"Any idea why he was there?"

Anton shook his head. "No clue. A stalker, perhaps. Lacey had one last year, remember?"

"You mean the guy you put in the hospital?"

"He fell."

"Sure he did." Mike smiled. "Right into your fist."

"He was in her dressing room going through her things when she walked in on him. I heard her scream and responded. Simple as that."

"That was one hell of a response. As I recall, you broke three fingers on his right hand and his wrist."

"It could have been worse."

"For him or you?"

"I don't take particularly well to someone coming at me with a knife. He got in a good swipe. Caught me in the arm. I think I may have gone a little nuts on him after that."

"Punctured lung. Dislocated shoulder. Busted knee cap. Shattered orbital bone. Did I miss anything?"

Anton smirked. "A broken nose and three fractured ribs."

"I still say he got off easy," Mike replied. "You saved Lacey's life that night. You know that, right? Remember what the cops said?"

Anton nodded. “They found an abduction kit in his car. Duct tape, rope, three more knives.”

“And that if you hadn’t taken him out when you did, they were sure he would have killed her.”

“I was just doing my job.”

“Baloney. You don’t believe that for a second.”

“Excuse me?”

“You’re meant to be in Lacey’s life.”

“What do you mean?”

“You’re her guardian angel, pal. Only live and in the flesh.”

“You’re not going to go all existential on me now, are you?”

“Hey man, the facts are the facts. We’re all interconnected. Call it a spirit thing or whatever. But we all play a role in each other’s lives, some bigger than others. Yours is to protect Lacey. How else do you explain it?”

“Explain what?”

“That this is the second time you’ve come to her defense when someone’s tried to harm her. It could have been anyone, but it wasn’t. It was you.”

“I’ve done nothing to help her yet.”

“You mean besides trying to track her down and taking a baseball bat to the head for your trouble? I’d say that kind of qualifies.”

“You’re being dramatic,” Anton said. “Can’t you just pass the time talking about sports like a normal person?”

“Admit it, tough guy. The two of you are meant to be together.”

“What if that’s for a bad reason and not a good one? What if I’m drawing danger to her instead of protecting her?”

"I'm not buying it. You're too much of a goody-goody. Besides, Lacey is nuts about you."

"Yeah, right."

"You don't believe me? Ask Shona-Lee. All Lacey does is talk about you."

"She does?"

"From the second she walks into the club. She's got the hots for you, man."

Anton smiled. The news lifted his spirits. "Where are we headed?"

"Back to the Odyssey. We need to meet with Russ."

"Did this private investigator get an address when he ran the plate?"

"Of course."

"Did it come back to a business or a private residence?"

"Business. Why?"

"Then that's where we're going."

"But Russ made it clear—"

"I don't give a damn what Russ said," Anton said sharply. "Lacey is our priority. For all we know the guy is going after her right now. We need to check out that address. What's the name of the company?"

"Kessel's Bookbinding and Restoration."

"Then that's where we're going."

Degario sighed. "Okay. Just do me a favor?"

"What's that?"

"Say something nice about me at my funeral, because Russ is gonna kill me for doing this."

"I'll handle Russ," Anton replied. "Just step on it."

# 20

AROUND THE CORNER from the Odyssey Gentlemen's Club, the agents found the domicile of the man Shona-Lee Cairns referred to as Father Frank Who Lives Under the Bridge. More to the point, Father Frank found them standing several feet in front of Biscuit. The snarling German Shepherd was wound up, hackles raised, standing his ground, in full defense mode, ready to protect his shanty home and master from the unannounced visitors. Agent Penner opened his jacket and placed his hand on his gun.

"That would be just about the worst thing you could do right now," Father Frank said. "Biscuit here is ex-military, like me. He knows guns. Given the three feet between you and him, the second I give the word he'll have torn your hand from that gun before you even come close to releasing the holster lock."

Penner took his hand off the Glock, showed the man his open hands. "Nice doggy," he said. He placed his hands on his hips. "I'm not a fan of dogs," he said.

"That's fine," Father Frank said. "Biscuit doesn't appear

to be overly thrilled to meet you either. And I find him to be an excellent judge of character." He looked the agents up and down. "Just who the hell are you and what do you want?"

Jordan spoke. "Mr. Paley, my name is Special Agent Jordan Quest. I'm with the FBI. These are my colleagues, Agents Penner and Hanover. May we have a minute of your time?"

Father Frank looked back at Penner, pointed to Jordan. "At least this one has manners," he said. "You, I'm not so sure about."

Max Penner looked at Chris as if to ask, *what did I do?* Chris smiled.

Biscuit continued to growl. Frank made no attempt to relax the dog. "How do you know my name?"

Jordan looked at Biscuit. The German Shepherd cocked its head. "May I?" she asked.

Father Frank warned. "I wouldn't if I were—"

Jordan stepped forward, took the dog's head in her hands, massaged Biscuit's ears, stroked his neck and chest. "Hey, baby," she said. "Who's a good boy?"

Biscuit's growl reduced to a whimper. He panted heavily, then calmed down, sat, and whined complacently.

"You've got quite a way with animals, Agent Quest," Father Frank said.

Jordan smiled. "We understand each other. If I don't see him as a threat, he won't see me as a threat."

"So it seems."

"I understand you dropped off an envelope at the Odyssey Club two days ago," Jordan said. "It was addressed to a woman by the name of Lacey Chastain. Do you remember?"

Father Frank shrugged. "What if I did?"

Chris interjected. "The woman works at the Odyssey. She's been reported missing."

"And you're telling me this why?"

Agent Penner jumped into the conversation. "We want to know how you came to be in possession of the envelope."

Father Frank smiled. "What's it worth to you?"

Penner turned to Chris. "Is he kidding me?"

"I'd say he's dead serious," Chris replied.

Penner stared at the man. "Do you realize I could charge you with interfering with a police investigation?"

"Do I look like I care?" Father Frank replied. "Besides, you won't."

"Really?" Penner said. "And why is that?"

"Because then there'd be a snowball's chance in hell of me ever telling you what you want to know. A hundred ought to do it."

"Didn't you hear what I--" Penner said.

"One-fifty."

"Not happening."

"You drive a hard bargain, Agent Penner," Father Frank said. "Why don't we make it an even two hundred?"

Jordan stood. Biscuit wagged his tail and pushed his head against her hand, prodding her to continue the attention. "Sir, we really need to know," she said. "A young woman's life may be at stake. I would appreciate anything you could tell us."

Father Frank held Penner's stare as he spoke to Jordan. "See? That's how you talk to someone. Just because I live on the street doesn't mean you can talk to me like something that just fell off your shoe. You, Agent Asshole, can go fuck yourself." He turned to Jordan. "Agent Quest, I'll be happy to provide you with whatever information you need."

"Thank you, sir," Jordan said.

Frustrated, Penner walked away. Biscuit growled. Jordan calmed the dog once again. "What can you tell me about the envelope?"

Father Frank looked over his shoulder and pointed. "Someone slipped it under my door, quiet as hell. Didn't even disturb Biscuit. Some guard dog, huh?"

Jordan smiled. "I'd say Agent Penner would disagree with you on that one."

"That's different," Father Frank said. "With guys like him, Biscuit and I both tend to get our backs up."

"And you didn't see who delivered it to you?"

"Haven't got a clue. But there were two envelopes, not one."

"Two?"

Father Frank nodded. "One was marked as you said it was. The other contained two-hundred bucks and a note that read, 'For Your Trouble.'"

"Do you still have that note?"

"Nah." He pointed to a trash can on the street corner. "I threw it in there. The city has probably emptied the bin by now."

"We'll have a look just the same."

Father Frank stroked Biscuit's head. "I'm sorry I couldn't be of more help."

"It's no problem," Jordan said. She shook Father Frank's hand. "I appreciate it just the same."

"Anything else I can help you with?"

"No, sir," Jordan said. "I think we're done here."

"All right," Father Frank replied. "Then if it's all the same to you, I'll take Biscuit inside. He's had a long walk. It's time for his snack."

Jordan took one-hundred dollars out of her purse and handed it to the man. "This is for you and Biscuit, from me," she said. "It's a personal gift, not a handout. Consider it my way of saying thanks for helping us with our investigation. Maybe you can take Biscuit out for dinner. Treat him to a steak."

Father Frank took the cash. "Thank you, ma'am," he said. "I appreciate that very much. So does Biscuit." He smiled. "We'll take you up on that suggestion."

"Good," Jordan said. "We'll be on our way, Father Frank. You and Biscuit take care of each another, okay?"

"Yes, ma'am. We sure will."

Jordan patted the dog on the head. "Be a good boy, Biscuit. Take care of your dad."

Biscuit wagged his tail and chuffed.

Jordan and Chris left the vagrant and walked down the street towards the trash can. Penner joined them.

"You want to search the can for that note?" Chris asked.

"Yeah," Jordan said. "And one more thing."

"What's that?" Chris asked.

"We need to place Father Frank under surveillance."

"Why?"

"Because he's lying through his teeth."

# 21

LACEY PULLED THE toolbox out of Victoria's cell and rummaged through it.

"What are you looking for?" Bonnie asked.

"Solder paste and matches."

"What for?"

"To blow the lock."

"Who are you?" Bonnie asked. "*Jane* Bond?"

Lacey smiled. "My father was a plumber. As a kid, I was a tomboy. I followed him everywhere he went. He taught me all about plumbing. The pay's great but the hours are terrible. He taught me how to solder a joint perfectly. And he also warned me about the dangers of the chemical components I was working with."

"Like solder?"

Lacey nodded. "The aluminum powder in solder, in particular." She found a can of paste, pulled it out of the box and handed it to Bonnie as she searched for the butane lighter. "Flip it over. Read the label," she said.

Bonnie read aloud the information on the underside of

the can. “Warning. Keep container closed. Under certain conditions, this product can ignite and/or explode.”

“Exactly,” Lacey said as she pulled the lighter from the box. “And we’re about to create the conditions for it to do precisely that.”

“How?” Bonnie asked.

“Solder is packed with particles of aluminum that have a very low flash point. When heated and exposed to oxygen they love to burn. I’m going to pack the lock full of both cans of paste, then set fire to it. Aluminum powder burns as fast as gunpowder and can ignite just as quickly. The powder in this product has a very small particle size, probably four-hundred-and-twenty microns or fewer. Thus, the reason for the fire and explosion hazard warning.”

Bonnie shook her head. “You know you’re my worst nightmare, right? Beautiful *and* brilliant.”

Lacey smiled. “Thanks, I think. I’d hold off on the brilliant part until I get us out of here. Can you find me a strip of medical gauze? I need to make a wick.”

“You’ve got it.”

While Bonnie searched the medical supplies closet for the gauze, Lacey removed the can of spray lubricant from the toolbox, walked up the staircase to the door, sprayed the frame of the door with the solvent, then opened the can of aluminum solder and spread the thick paste into the doorjamb and around the lock.

Bonnie met her at the top of the stairs with the gauze. Lacey handed her the can of penetrating oil. “Soak it in this,” she said, “then pack as much as you can into the gaps in the door frame, bottom, top and sides. When this thing starts to burn it’s going to get crazy in here real fast.”

Bonnie jammed the oil-drenched strips of medical dressing around the door as instructed.

"Perfect," Lacey said. The door had been completely sealed with the flammable mixture of solder paste and lubricant. "We'll need a long strip of gauze," she told Bonnie. "Roll out a section from here to the foot of the stairs, then get Melinda and Victoria around the corner. When this thing goes up, it will either explode, catch fire, or both."

"What if the fire spreads to the staircase before we can get out?" Bonnie asked. "We'll be trapped down here. We'll be burned alive."

"I won't let that happen."

"But what if it does?"

"Then who cares? If we can't get out of here, then we're dead already. It's only a matter of time before he comes back and kills us. Do you really want that animal to take your body apart, layer by layer?"

"You're right," Bonnie said. "I'd rather die down here, with all of you, taking a stand and fighting for my life than let him touch me ever again."

"No one's going to die today," Lacey said. She tied the end of the long strip of material around the doorknob and handed the roll of gauze and the can of lubricant to Bonnie. "Keep soaking it as you walk down the stairs. I'll be right down."

Bonnie unraveled the white medical dressing as she walked down the stairs, then moved Melinda and Victoria to safety.

Lacey called out. "Everyone clear?"

Bonnie replied. "All clear."

Lacey stared at the mass of medical gauze jammed into the doorframe. The top of the stairs reeked with the smell of penetrating oil and solder as rivers of the noxious mixture dripped down through cracks in the wooden door. She stared at the long wick that lay on the steps leading down to the room that was their prison. "This better work," she said.

Lacey walked down the steps and joined Bonnie, Victoria, and Melinda. The four women stood safely around the corner. She lit the butane lighter. "Ready?" she asked.

The women nodded.

"Here goes," Lacey said. She lit the makeshift wick and stood back.

Ignition was instantaneous. The oil-soaked length of medical dressing dissolved in a rush of smoke and fire as it slithered up the staircase, self-disintegrating as it jumped to the first step then struck out at the next, until it had traveled to the top of the stairs and met the frame of the door. With a tremendous *boom!* the door exploded. Cinders of burning wood fell onto the steps and floor below.

Lacey looked around the corner. The door was gone. In its place light beamed into the room from the top of the stairs.

They were free.

"Wait here," Lacey said. She ran to the toolbox, grabbed a hammer, and handed it to Bonnie. To Melinda and Victoria, she handed each a chisel. "For your protection," she said. "If he's up there and tries to stop us we kill him before he kills us. Agreed?"

The women nodded.

"What about you?" Victoria asked. "You're unarmed."

"I'd love for him to believe that," Lacey said. "I can take care of myself. It's you guys I'm worried about."

"Don't be," Victoria said. Her voice was cold. This was not the shrinking violet that only minutes ago had given up on surviving before climbing out of her cage to freedom. "I want him to be there." She gripped the screwdriver tightly in her hand. "I *need* him to be there. This will only be over for me when I see him dead. And I want to be the one to kill him."

"First things first, Vicky," Lacey said. She placed her hands on the woman's shoulders. Victoria was shaking with fear, fueled by adrenaline. "We get out of here and call the police."

"And then?" Melinda asked.

Leading their ascent to freedom, Lacey headed towards the staircase. "Then we turn the tables on the sonofabitch."

## 22

ON THE STREET corner, Chris rifled through the trash can, searching for the envelope and note Father Frank said he had discarded.

"What did you find out, Jordan?" he asked. "What makes you believe Father Frank is lying?"

"Something I felt when I shook his hand," Jordan replied. "He was thinking about Lacey. He knows her."

"Why wouldn't he?" Penner said. "Shona-Lee Cairns told us Russ Paley lets him and Biscuit stay at the club when the weather's bad. He would likely have met her at one time or another."

"He was being purposely evasive," Chris said. "Jordan told him Lacey had been reported missing. Mentioned her by name. Father Frank did not even let on that he knew her name. Which Jordan knows is not true. The envelope we found in her locker -the one he delivered to the club- was addressed to her."

"It's more than that," Jordan said. "I felt a connection between him and Scroll."

"You think he knows who Scroll is?"

"He definitely knows more than he's letting on."

"Then what are we waiting for?" Agent Penner said. "Let's go back and take his ass into custody, bring him in for questioning."

"We can't do that," Jordan said. "We have no evidence. It'll be my word against his. He'll lawyer up, ask for a public defender, and that will be it. We'll lose him. Which means we'll lose any shot we have of using him to find Scroll."

"So we're back to surveillance," Penner said.

"It's our best bet for now," Jordan said.

Chris pulled the last few scraps of paper out of the bottom of the trash can. Stuck to a crumpled envelope was a length of red string. "I may have something," he said. The agent unfolded the envelope. The calligraphy on the front read, 'For Your Trouble.'

"Found it," Chris said. He opened the envelope carefully. "There's a note inside," he said.

"What does it say?" Penner asked.

"Jesus!" Chris said as he handed Penner the note. He read it aloud. "It's time. Set it up." The agent deduced the meaning of the message. "Father Frank doesn't just know Lacey. He's working with Scroll."

Chris was already on the run with Jordan hot on his heels. He yelled back to Penner as the two agents headed for Father Frank's domicile under the bridge. "Call it in!"

Outside the tarpaulin-draped entrance to Father Frank's, Jordan and Chris drew their weapons. Chris raised his arm, made a fist, and glanced at Max Penner as he caught up. Heeding the request for a silent approach, Penner took a position ten feet back, raised his gun, and waited for Jordan and Chris to initiate contact with the man who had instantly become a person of interest in their investigation.

Chris nodded at Jordan, an acknowledgement that she

should be first to communicate with Father Frank with whom, it seemed, she had developed a rapport.

Jordan called out. "Father Frank? It's Agent Quest. I have a couple more questions for you if you don't mind. Would that be all right?"

No response.

Jordan tried again to reach out to the vagrant. "I only need another moment of your time, Father Frank."

Silence.

Chris shook his head. He looked back at Penner and indicated he and his partner would be moving forward. Penner acknowledged the plan. To Jordan, Chris mouthed his instructions: "On three."

Jordan nodded.

One... two... *three.*

Chris threw back the tarpaulin and stepped inside Father Frank's shanty. "FBI!" he yelled. Jordan moved in behind him. Penner held his position momentarily, then followed the agents into the habitat.

The shanty was empty.

Father Frank and Biscuit were gone.

"Good God," Penner muttered as he holstered his weapon. "What the hell is this?"

The walls of the homeless man's home were wallpapered with newspaper articles. Penner read the headlines: HUDSON RIVER HORROR... CITY UNDER SIEGE... BODY COUNT RISES... SCROLL KILLER TAUNTS NYPD... TENTH VICTIM FOUND... CARNAGE IN CENTRAL PARK... WHO IS THE SCROLL KILLER?... NIGHTMARE IN NEW YORK... MAYOR SCULLIA TO TASK FORCE: FIND SCROLL!

Chris said, "Either Father Frank has taken an abnormal level of interest in this case..."

"This isn't abnormal interest," Jordan said. "This, for lack of a better way of putting it, is a shrine."

"You were right," Penner said. "Father Frank is involved."

There was barely enough room for the agents to move past one another in the small space. Overhead, passing cars rattled soup cans stacked high on a metal shelf. Biscuit's porcelain water bowl clattered on the asphalt floor.

"He knew we'd be coming back," Chris said. "He must have left with the dog seconds after we walked away."

"He won't be difficult to find," Penner said. "A vagrant traveling with a German Shepherd is hard to miss."

"Father Frank and Biscuit are staples in this neighborhood," Jordan said. "There's a good chance people won't believe he's connected to Scroll. They'll protect them first, even hide them. Father Frank already lives off the grid. No permanent address, cellphone, nothing. He probably knows a million places to disappear in this city if he wants to. We need to contact Commissioner Haley. Get him to order uniforms to canvas the area and ask around, maybe get a lead on his whereabouts."

"How much you want to bet the guy and his dog are already ghosts?" Chris said.

Jordan ran her fingertips over the newspaper articles. Scenes from each of the murders played in her mind.

To Penner, she said, "Call in a forensics team. I want every one of these articles taken back to the office. I need to spend time with these documents. I think they can tell us how to find Scroll."

# 23

OTTO TAPPED ON the privacy partition and spoke to the cab driver. "Let me out," he said.

"But we're still twenty minutes away," the cabbie said.

"I know," Otto said. "I have an errand to run."

"You sure you want me to let you out here?"

"Pull over."

The driver shrugged. "Whatever you say."

Otto paid the driver, watched him speed away, walked to the back of the apartment building, looked up. The children's cries fell from an open window on the seventh floor. He had been watching the building for some time; particularly the comings and goings of the woman he had been tracking for the past two weeks. He could hear her yelling at the top of her lungs for the children to be quiet. He learned she had seven young ones, of varying ages, from different fathers. Her name was Rosalita "Loba" Sanchez. Known as The Wolf, she was the most feared and ruthless drug lord in New York City.

In conducting his background research on Rosalita, he

learned she had worked with her connections in Columbia to establish a cocaine distribution system that was the envy of the Medellin drug cartel. She could have lived well in New York, easily afforded any of the many multi-million-dollar penthouse suites the city had to offer. But she came from the streets, the slums of Juarez, and it was among the dirt and filth and cockroaches that she felt most at home.

Otto made her sentries the second he stepped out of the cab; four thugs, stupid enough to believe that by wearing gang colors and slinging dope out in the open they would not call attention to themselves. Police spent little time in this neighborhood. There was no point. It had become a cesspool of criminal activity. He felt eyes on him.

"Rosalita home?" Otto asked.

Surprised to know he had been seen peering around the corner, the kid stepped out into the open. "Who's askin?"

"A friend," Otto replied without turning around.

"Loba's friends use the front door," the kid said. "And only if we say so."

Otto turned. "We haven't seen one another for quite a while," he lied. "I doubt she'd even recognize me."

"Then that wouldn't make you her friend, would it?"

Otto smiled. "It's important that I see her. We have unfinished business."

The kid put one hand behind his back. Otto knew what that meant. "This ain't no place for you, mister," the kid said. "Go home while you can still walk."

"I'm afraid I can't do that," Otto replied. "Will you please do me a favor?"

"Leave. Now."

Otto continued. "I need you to go upstairs and ask Rosalita to call a sitter for the children. What we have to discuss is not suitable for tender ears."

The kid removed the gun from his back, held it at his side. "Where you want it?" he said.

"Trust me, son," Otto said as he removed his backpack. "You don't want to do this. I've already been shot once today." He showed the kid his bloody, wounded shoulder. "Twice would really piss me off."

The kid was cold. "That scratch?" he said. "Let me show you what a real hole looks like." As he raised the gun a glint of light caught his eye. The blade sailed through the air, caught him in his throat, buried itself deep. Wide-eyed, dumbfounded at the instantaneous counterattack, the kid fell to his knees, dropped the gun. The weapon clattered on the ground beside him. He tried to breathe, gurgled instead.

Otto walked up to him, put his hand on the blade, turned it quickly. The light in the kid's eyes faded. "You should have checked me for a weapon, dumbass," he said. He wrenched out the knife, cleaned it on the kid's shirt, then returned it to its secret sheath on the back of his knapsack.

He pulled the kid's dead body out of the middle of the alleyway, dragged it around the corner, leaned it against the wall, placed the gun in his hand.

Eventually he would be found.

No one would care.

One less drug-dealing punk to worry about.

A cockroach of a different kind.

With his shoulder wounded, accessing the fire ladder on the side of the building proved to be difficult. Otto grabbed the access rung and pulled hard. The section lowered to the ground with a clang. He looked up, wary of the noise he had made, stayed under the ladder, out of sight, and waited. All clear. Slowly, he ascended the ladder to Rosalita's balcony on the seventh floor. The children were screaming as too was Rosalita. Otto stepped onto the balcony and peered into the apartment.

The woman's seven children were seated on the floor. The smell of urine and feces wafting out through the window assaulted his senses to such a degree he thought he might wretch. The reason for the children's cried were obvious now. Rosalita had left them sitting in their own filth.

Some people were meant to die.

Rosalita Sanchez was one such person.

Otto slipped into the living room through the open window, drew his knife from his backpack, moved quickly through the apartment and surprised Rosalita in her bathroom. The drug lord was preparing to sample a line of her own product when he burst through the door, slit her throat with the knife, then threw her body in the bathtub and cut open her stomach.

Hundreds of dime bags of cocaine, prepared for sale, were stacked on bathroom shelves around her.

Otto shoved the drugs into her stomach cavity, packing the woman as full of the deadly product as her small frame would permit, then broke open several of the bags and shook them over her body. The powder fell on her face, arms, and hands. Satisfied he had made a suitable example out of her, he stood back and observed his work.

Everything had gone exactly as planned.

He was proud of himself. If killing was an artform, he was Picasso.

The military had taught him well.

He retrieved his favorite quill pen from the backpack, dipped it in her blood, withdrew a section of skin he had previously harvested and cured, and crafted a beautiful note:

. . .

*Dear Commissioner Haley,*

*Today I give you the Wolf and her seven young cubs.*

*The children are innocent.*

*The woman is not.*

*This is the start.*

*There will be more.*

*You're welcome.*

He rolled the note into a scroll, bound it with a length of red ribbon, and shoved it up Rosalita's left nostril.

Otto left the apartment as silently as he had entered it, but not before picking up Rosalita's cellphone from the kitchen counter and placing a call.

"NYPD. How may I direct your call?"

"Office of the Commissioner, please."

"One moment."

Otto wiped the phone with a dishtowel, set it down, slipped out through the window to the fire escape and descended the ladder.

The kid's body had not been disturbed. Par for the neighborhood, he thought.

Back on the street he hailed a cab. "Manhattan," he told the driver.

"Yes, sir."

In Rosalita Sanchez's apartment, repeated requests for the caller's identity went unanswered.

As the taxicab sped away from the curb Otto knew the call was already being traced, the police dispatched. The children would be found. Child Protective Services would intervene. Perhaps one day each of them would find a safe and happy home. He thought about the alternative and came to a simple conclusion: better to be a ward of the state than a cub in Sanchez's pack.

## 24

LACEY AND BONNIE reached the top of the stairs with Melinda and Victoria following close behind. Sections of the blown-out doorframe had caught fire. Lacey kicked what remained of the door off its hinges. The cinders fell into the hallway.

"Stay close," Lacey said. "If you see him, hit first and ask questions later."

"That won't be a problem," Victoria answered.

The corridor was dark. Down the hall, the outline of a second door. Light permeated through cracks in its frame.

"There's a room ahead," Bonnie said.

"Wait here," Lacey said. "I'll check it out first."

"Be careful," Bonnie warned.

Lacey crept toward the darkened doorway, placed her hand on the doorknob, tested it.

She expected the door to be locked. Instead, the knob turned freely.

Lacey opened the door. The room was full of books stacked on benches and shelves in various states of repair. She looked over her shoulder. "All clear," she said as she stepped through the door into the room. The women joined her.

"My God," Bonnie said as she looked around. She picked up several of the leather-bound books, put them down. "I know this place."

"You've been here before?" Lacey asked.

Bonnie nodded. "Many times. This is Kessel's."

"What the hell is Kessel's?" Lacey asked.

Melinda answered the question. "Kessel's Bookbinding and Restoration."

"One of the largest companies of its kind in New York City," Victoria added. "Probably even the country."

"You *all* know it?" Lacey asked.

"Mrs. Kessel runs the store," Vicky said. "Has for decades."

"You mean ran the store," Bonnie corrected.

"How's that?" Lacey asked.

"She died a year ago. As far as I know no one has taken over the business. I would have known about it if they had. My company was the main supplier to Kessel's for everything when it came to book restoration. Paper, leather, antique writing instruments... you name it. Mrs. Kessel was a legend in the industry, especially coming from such a famous family."

"Famous how?" Lacey asked.

"Her great-grandfather was Jacob Grimm. His brother was Wilhelm."

The news stunned Lacey. "As in the Brothers Grimm? Grimm's Fairy Tales?"

"The same."

"Holy crap."

Melinda asked, "If the shop has been closed, how the

hell did we end up here? And what was she doing with a dungeon in her basement?"

Vicky walked to the front door of the establishment and removed a sign from inside the window. She held it up for the others to see. The sign read UNDER NEW MANAGEMENT. OPENING SOON. "Someone bought the place."

Lacey lifted the telephone handset from its wall-mounted cradle, listened for a dial tone. "Phone's dead," she said. "Line's been turned off."

Phantom images swept back and forth in front of the white-washed front windows. "No one can see into the shop from outside," Melinda remarked. "As far as anyone knows the place is vacant." She scratched a pane of white-washed glass with her fingernail. Rays of sunlight slashed into the establishment and brightened the dull room. She unlocked the front door deadbolt and turned the knob. The heavy door squeaked opened. Melanie stepped outside, soon joined by the others.

The sounds and smells of the city filled the air.

They were free.

At the intersection, across the street, a NYPD patrol car waited for the signal light to turn green.

"Come on," Lacey said.

Together the women raced to the squad car.

WITHIN MINUTES, the normally quiet intersection was bustling with emergency personnel as two additional police units and three ambulances arrived on the scene.

While Melinda and Victoria gave their statements to police, Bonnie was transferred to a gurney in the back of the ambulance and began receiving the professional medical attention she so desperately needed. Lacey sat beside her and held her hand. "We would never have made it out of there if it hadn't been for you," Bonnie told her new friend. "You're amazing."

"Nah, just beautiful and brilliant," Lacey teased, reminding her of her earlier compliment. "You're the one who's amazing. To go through what you did and not come out of this a basket case is nothing short of incredible."

"Who says I'm not?" Bonnie admitted. "Every time I close my eyes, all I can see is his damn mask and hear his voice. I'm not nearly as together as you think I am."

Lacey squeezed her hand. "You'll be fine. I'm going with you to the hospital. Is there someone I can call to meet us there?"

Bonnie nodded. Tears welled in her eyes. "My husband, Owen."

"I'll see to it he's there when we arrive."

"Thank you."

"Sorry to interrupt," the paramedic said as he climbed into the back of the ambulance. "How's my patient doing?"

Bonnie forced a smile. "Okay, I guess," she replied.

"Don't let her fool you," Lacey said. "This one's tough as nails."

The paramedic placed a blood pressure cuff around Bonnie's arm, checked her vitals. "From what I hear about the ordeal you've been through I don't doubt that for a minute," he said. He released the pressure. The bladder hissed as it deflated. "BP's one-thirty over ninety," he said. "Under the circumstances, that's pretty good." He shuffled out of the ambulance. To Lacey he said, "We'll be leaving any minute. You can ride with your friend."

"Thanks," Lacey replied. She smiled. "You coming too?"

The paramedic blushed. "I have to," he said. "I'm driving."

"I feel better already," Lacey teased.

Lacey caught him looking back at her as he walked away. She smiled at Bonnie. "Did you notice if he was wearing a ring?"

Bonnie coughed as she laughed. "Only you could think about picking up a guy at a time like this."

"That man can take my temperature anytime. And I'm not particularly fussy where he wants to take it."

"You're too much."

The paramedic returned to his ambulance and checked on his patient. "The hospital's waiting for us. You two all set for transport?"

Lacey smiled. "Take me anywhere you want," she replied.

The paramedic laughed. "Maybe I should just call you a cab. You look absolutely fine to me."

"No," Lacey said. "I feel faint." She placed her hand dramatically against her forehead. "Yes, most definitely weak. Very weak. If I pass out, promise me you'll bring me back."

"That shouldn't be a problem."

"I'd prefer mouth-to-mouth."

"I'll see what I can do." The paramedic smiled as he closed the doors.

ACROSS THE STREET from Kessel's, Otto's cab slowed to a stop. He recognized the two women standing beside the police car.

How the hell had they escaped?

Where were the others?

The ambulance turned on its lights and drove down the adjoining back alley.

"That'll be seventy bucks," the driver said.

"Keep going," Otto said.

Confused, the driver asked, "Isn't this where you said you wanted to go?"

"I changed my mind. Drive."

Nonplussed, the cabbie pulled away from the curb. "Whatever you say, mister. It's your dime. Where to next?" he asked.

"Anywhere but here," Otto replied.

# 25

FATHER FRANK WAS in a panic.

Otto took the call as the cab driver rounded the corner from Kessel's. The number on the display was unknown. He opened the line, said nothing, waited for the caller to speak.

"You there?" the caller asked.

Otto recognized the voice. "Why are you calling me?"

"The cops were here," Father Frank said. "Asked about the note you gave me to give to the girl."

"What did you tell them?"

"Nothing."

Otto didn't reply.

"*Nothing*," Father Frank repeated. "I didn't tell them a damn thing. I said someone slipped the note under the tarp and that I took the money and did as I was instructed to do. That's it." Father Frank was angry. "You said this would be simple, that you had it all figured out. Now I've got nowhere to go. The police are all over my place. I'm burned."

"Is the dog with you?"

"Biscuit? Of course."

"Lose it."

"What?"

"Get rid of the dog. You need to disappear. It's only going to slow you down."

"But Biscuit needs..."

"I don't give a shit what the fucking dog needs," Otto said. "Ask yourself a simple question, Frank."

"What?" he asked.

"Do you want to go down for this or not? Because you're as neck deep in it as I am."

Father Frank was near tears at the thought of having to give up his precious Biscuit. "No," he replied.

"No what?"

"No, I don't."

"Damn right," Otto said. "Now get yourself together and listen. Can you make your way uptown?"

"I don't know. The FBI's looking for me. Which means so is NYPD."

"You need to go underground," Otto said. "I have someone I can contact who can get you to me. We'll leave the city. We've made our mark here. Maybe we'll head to Detroit or Chicago. Start fresh."

"Miami," Father Frank said. "I want to go back to Miami. I hate the cold."

"Fine," Otto replied. "Miami it is. I take it you're calling from a payphone?"

"Yes."

"You still have the money I gave you?"

"Some of it, yeah."

"Buy a burner phone. And don't call from the street. You're way too hot right now to expose yourself."

"Where are you?"

"Around."

"You can't afford to take any chances either. You need to get off the radar too."

"It's you I'm concerned about. No one knows who I am. But you... you're radioactive."

"I won't talk."

"I know you won't. You know the consequences if you do."

"Don't threaten me, Otto. I said I won't talk."

"Every man has a breaking point, Frank. Do you know yours?"

"I know what's in store for me if we're caught," Father Frank replied. "I'm not going to spend the rest of my life in prison for what we've done."

"No one's going to prison," Otto said. "The cops are clued out. Relax, Frank. Everything will be fine. Now go to a convenience store and buy the phone. Call me when you have it. I'll arrange for your pick up shortly."

"All right."

Otto hung up the phone, placed a call.

"Hudson Sanitation and Waste Disposal."

"I'd like to order a pickup," Otto said.

"Account number?"

"I don't have one, but I hear it's hot in California today."

The caller paused. "Hold on."

Otto waited. The man returned to the line a few seconds later. "Yes, but the surfing is good."

"Especially in Big Sur."

"Best waves on the West Coast," the man replied.

"We good?" Otto asked.

"Yeah," the man confirmed, satisfied that the caller was legitimate. "What do you need?"

"One package for pickup and disposal."

"Where?"

"Manhattan."

"When?"

"Now."

"Location?"

"That's pending. He's gone dark for the moment."

"You want us to be in the area when he shows up?"

"That would be ideal."

"Done. We're rolling a truck. Call back when you have the details." The man hung up.

Otto's phone rang. A different number appeared on screen. He picked up.

"Got it," Frank said.

"Good. Where are you now?"

"Pick 'n Go Convenience. A few blocks from the Odyssey."

"Wait around the back, behind the garbage disposal," Otto said. "I'm sending someone to get you. You won't recognize them, but they'll recognize you. When they ask, tell them 'the best waves are in Big Sur.'"

"All right. And Otto?"

"Yes?"

"I meant what I said."

"About?"

"I won't talk. Not to the cops, not to anyone."

"I know you won't, Frank. I believe you. I trust you."

"Good," Frank replied. "It's important to me that you do."

"Stay put," Otto said. "Everything will be fine. Hang in there. You won't have to wait long. Thirty minutes, tops."

"All right."

"I know you're scared. Don't be. Everything is under control."

"Okay."

"Go."

Father Frank disconnected the call.

Otto called Hudson Sanitation and Disposal once more. He didn't bother with the cryptic formalities. "It's me. Go to the Pick 'n Go Convenience, two blocks from the Odyssey Gentlemen's Club. The package is behind the Dumpster."

"We know the place. You want the usual service?"

"That will be fine."

"We're on our way. Want us to call when it's done?"

"That won't be necessary," Otto said. "I won't be available."

"Nice doing business with you." The man hung up.

Otto placed his phone in his pocket. He needed to think.

By now the police would be going through Kessel's with a fine-tooth comb. They would have found the dungeon, but that would be all they would find. He had been careful. No trace of Scroll had been left behind. The women weren't a problem either. He had always worn a masquerade mask in their presence and used a vocal scrambler when he spoke. They would have no clue as to his identity.

Otto felt good about himself. He had always been a meticulous planner. The abductions were no different. The same care and attention to detail had gone into the kidnapping and subsequent elimination of his victims as the interrogations he had conducted overseas.

Soon Hudson Sanitation would deal with his Father Frank problem.

Otto pressed his palm against the passenger window of the cab. It was sunny and hot outside.

Like the weather, his day had improved immensely.

## 26

IN THE SHANTY, Father Frank's only belongings consisted of a foldable army-surplus military cot and pillow, a propane cooking stove and spare gas cylinder, several pots and pans, canned and box foods, several bottles of water, half a can of Folgers coffee, a bag of dry dog food, a change of clothes and a well-worn blanket. The blanket lay on the floor beside his bed in the tiny domicile and no doubt served as Biscuit's bed. Chris found a knife hidden under the pillow, likely placed there for quick access and personal protection. He handed it to Jordan and pointed out the crimson flecks that speckled the blade.

"Could be blood," he said.

Jordan turned the knife in the light, examined it, then closed her eyes and connected. The scene flashed through her mind. Explosions all around... screaming... Father Frank dragging the knife across the man's neck, then driving it down into his shoulder... pulling it out, delivering a final thrust into the small of his back... then guiding the lifeless body to the ground.

"It is," Jordan said. "This knife was used to kill, but not to murder. It was used in combat."

"Father Frank told Penner he and Biscuit were ex-military."

Jordan nodded. "The energy in this place is very dark," she said, "but it's not Father Frank's. It's Scroll's. He's spent time here."

"We know they know each other," Chris said. "The note I found in the trash confirms it."

Jordan studied the newspaper articles on the wall, psychically reading the stories behind the murders, like the woman referred to in the article entitled 'BODY COUNT RISES,' found in the trunk of an abandoned car in Bedford-Stuyvesant, dressed in white, whose hands had been removed. Scroll's note stated that her death and the amputation of her extremities had been at the request of the Devil.

The next article, 'SCROLL KILLER TAUNTS NYPD' and its accompanying note had been reprinted in the New York Times:

*Dear Commissioner Haley,*

*Mating is a tiresome ritual, is it not?*
*You might even call it a process of 'elimination.'*
*Cinderella she was not.*
*One more down, many to go.*
*Wish me luck.*

The article further informed how the woman was found immaculately dressed yet without shoes in an alley, in Queens, heels slashed, toes removed, throat cut.

Jordan felt there was something familiar about the victimology. Was it possible she had crossed paths with this killer before?

*Many to go.*

He was out there, somewhere, killing at will and with a purpose. The notes were getting more specific. These were not random kills as the police had suspected.

Found without shoes, toes removed... *Cinderella*?

Jordan turned to her partner. "I think I might know what this is about."

"Feel free to clue me in," Chris answered.

"Fairy tales."

Chris looked puzzled. "What are you talking about?"

She pointed to the excerpt in the article. "He's serious when he refers to this being a process of elimination. I think he's looking for a particular person, someone he thinks is special. And when he realizes he hasn't found her he has no choice but to kill her. But he's doing so in very specific ways. The deaths seem scripted, like he's following a manual on the many ways to kill."

"Perfect," Chris replied. "Just what we need. A psychopath using the streets of New York to test his murder theories."

"This is beyond theory," Jordan said. "There's method to his madness. There's so much variance in the crimes. They don't fit a pattern. Perhaps that's the whole point. What if each of the murders is meant to be different, unique, one of a kind?"

"I don't follow."

"Work with me on this, okay?"

"I'm listening."

"We know that most serial killers follow the same modus operandi... method of operation. It becomes their signature. The BTK Killer would bind, torture, and kill. Jeffrey Dahmer cannibalized his victims. Zodiac's process was to shoot his victims in cars at close range and send the police an unbreakable cipher. Maybe Scroll's process is to make every kill different. Maybe *that's* his signature. The scrolls are his ciphers. He leaves them behind to call attention to the crimes. I'd be willing to bet the NYPD would never have attributed these murders to the same killer had it not been for the scrolls."

Chris nodded. "That's true. Courtney Valentine's body was disposed of in pieces, none of which were found at the actual crime scene. But the scroll was."

Jordan agreed. She pointed to the first and second articles. "In Bedford-Stuyvesant, he claims the woman's hands were removed at the request of the Devil. In the case of this victim, he chops away at her feet then disposes of her, referring to her as Cinderella. My guess is that when we look deeper into every one of these murders, the one thing they'll have in common is a bizarre set of circumstances relative to each of the deaths and the scroll found at the scene."

"That will make finding this guy hard as hell."

"Maybe not."

"What are you thinking?"

"That he's following a manual of murder, of sorts."

"What do you mean?"

"Did your parent's ever read you bedtime stories?"

"Of course."

"Mine too. When I was a kid, I loved fairy tales. One day my father read Grimm's Fairy Tales to me. My mother put an end to that in a hurry. She told him they were far too violent, which they were. They gave me nightmares. My mother hid the book."

"Let me guess. You searched for it, found it and read it."

Jordan smiled. "Cover to cover. Every last story. Which is why something felt familiar when I reviewed the case files. These murders are not random. I think he's recreating them from a book."

"Grimm's Fairy Tales?"

Jordan nodded. "Or one like it. Courtney Valentine's head was found with her long hair intact. The bag contained leaves. Do you know what kind they were?"

"Sorry, I failed botany. Haven't got a clue."

"Rapunzel leaves."

Chris got the connection. "As in Rapunzel, the fairy tale?"

"Yes," Jordan replied. "The victims in these stories fit the theory. There's a story called The Girl with No Hands, whose hands were cut off by her father to give to the Devil... just like the woman in Bed-Stuy. The woman found in the alley had no shoes and her feet had been mutilated, like he was trying to make a shoe *fit*, as in Cinderella. I think when he realized she wasn't the one he was looking for he killed her."

Chris crossed his arms. "This is one hell of a stretch, Jordan."

"Maybe," Jordan replied. "But everything in me is telling me I'm right."

Agent Penner interrupted. "You're not going to believe this," he said. "I got a phone call from Keon. Four women just identified themselves to NYPD as kidnap victims. One of them had layers of her skin removed. She's on her way to the hospital right now. How much do you want to bet they're connected to Scroll?"

"Which hospital?" Chris asked.

"Bellevue."

"Let's go," Jordan said.

## 27

ANTON JUMPED OUT of the car as Mike Degario pulled the limo to the curb. The police had cordoned off the street outside Kessel's Bookbinding and Restoration. Plainclothes officers walked in and out of the unassuming shop. Some carried boxes, others paper bags, all labeled EVIDENCE.

Anton ran to the police tape, lifted it, ducked under.

"Whoa!" a uniformed officer called out. "Where do you think you're going?" He grabbed Anton by the arm, held him back.

"Lacey Chastain," Anton said. There was panic in his voice. "Is she here? Is she all right?"

"Slow down a minute, mister," the officer said. "Catch your breath. Who is it you're asking for?"

Anton forced himself to calm down. The sight of the overwhelming police presence at Kessel's had gotten the better of him. "Lacey Chastain," he repeated.

"Who is she to you?"

"A friend," Anton said. He tried to step into the crime scene area, was stopped. "What happened here?"

"Police business," the officer replied. He took Anton by the arm and escorted him away from the barrier. "Now tell me who Lacey Chastain is and why you think she's here."

A voice called out from behind. "I've got this, officer." The man walked up. He wore a dark blue windbreaker with large gold letters on the sleeves that read NYPD. "My name is Detective Rick Pallister, NYPD Homicide. And you are?"

"Anton Moore, sir."

"What's with all the drama, Mr. Moore? You know something about what went down here?"

"Went down?"

"Come on, Mr. Moore. You know what I'm talking about. Citizens don't try to bust through police barriers without a damn good reason."

"I'm looking for a friend."

"Your friend doesn't have a phone? You can't just call her?"

"I'm sorry. I had reason to believe she might be here," Anton said. "I was wrong." He turned to leave.

Pallister stopped him. "Not so fast, Mr. Moore. We're not finished here." The detective grabbed him by his arm.

Anton looked at the cop's hand, then up at the detective. "Are you arresting me?" he asked.

"Do I need to?" Pallister asked.

"We both know that's an international sign of arrest," Anton said. "If you're not detaining me, then I suggest you let go of me."

Pallister released his grip. He studied Anton. "You're not a cop but you sure as hell look like one. Talk like one too."

"I work the door at the Odyssey," Anton said. "I provide protection for the dancers. That's who I'm looking for. One of the girls, Lacey Chastain. No one can reach her. I'm concerned for her safety."

"Fair enough. But why does that bring you here?"

"I visited her apartment this morning. Ran into a little trouble."

"What kind of trouble?"

"I'd rather not say."

"I'd rather you did."

"Let me put it this way," Anton said. "It didn't go so well. I'll probably be feeling the effects for the next couple of days."

"Someone assaulted you?"

"You could say that."

"You don't strike me as the kind of guy that someone gets the drop on easily."

"I'm not."

"What can you tell me about Lacey Chastain?" Pallister asked.

"Why do you want to know?"

"Because she's one of four victims whose case we're now investigating."

*Victim?* The word struck Anton hard as he heard it. He felt the blood rush out of his face, suddenly felt weak. "What... what happened?" he asked. "Is Lacey...?"

"Dead?" Pallister finished. "No, Mr. Moore. Quite the opposite. She's very much alive. From what we understand she's the reason they all survived."

"All? How many are we talking about?"

"Three other women. Seems like they'd been held here for some time. Your friend orchestrated their escape. They made themselves known to police. I'm here following up. You read the papers?"

"Of course," Anton said.

"Then you're aware of the Scroll Killer murders."

Anton nodded. "Who isn't?"

"We believe this is where he was keeping his victims. At least the ones he didn't kill."

"Did you catch him?"

"Not yet. But it's only a matter of time before we do."

"Where's Lacey now?" Anton asked.

"Accompanying one of the victims to Bellevue Hospital. I'm heading over there now. Want to join me?"

"Please."

"Maybe you can help us."

"Anything."

"Talk to Ms. Chastain when we get to Bellevue. Find out whatever you can about Scroll. He's not finished yet. We need to find him before anyone else gets hurt or killed."

"I'll do whatever I can to help, Detective."

"Thanks, Mr. Moore." Pallister offered his hand.

Anton shook it. "It's Anton."

The cop smiled. "Maybe on the way you can fill me in on everything you haven't told me so far."

Anton nodded. "That's a two-way street."

"Fair enough. You play your hand, I'll play mine."

"Deal," Anton said. "Give me a second. I need to talk to my friend."

"All right," Pallister said. "But we leave in five."

"I'll be right there."

MIKE DEGARIO STOOD beside the limo. "Lacey's safe," Anton explained. "She's at Bellevue. Detective Pallister and I are heading over there now."

"Detective Pallister?" Mike asked.

"He's with NYPD Homicide."

"Jesus Christ, Anton. What's the homicide unit doing here?"

"They think the Scroll Killer had Lacey."

"Are you friggin' kidding me? And she escaped?"

"Yeah. Listen Mike, I've gotta go. I'll fill you in later. Tell Russ to hold off on the cavalry for now. This situation is a lot heavier than we thought it was."

"All right. Just keep me in the loop, okay?"

Anton shook his friend's hand. "I will. Thanks, Mike. I'll be in touch."

# 28

FATHER FRANK HEARD the rumble of the garbage truck as it backed into the parking lot of the Pick 'n Go convenience store and hissed to a stop in front of the disposal bin behind which he had been told to hide. He remained out of sight, wary of the driver, unsure what to do next.

He peered around the corner, watched the cab door open and the driver step down. Another man, his passenger, jumped down from the truck, turned his back and watched the street.

Never had he felt so defenseless. In his rush to leave the shanty he had left his knife under his pillow. He had placed Biscuit in the care of Brooklyn Bob, his only friend in the city of makeshift dwellings. The old man loved Biscuit as much as he did. He knew the dog would be safe and in good hands. Perhaps one day when he and Otto had resettled in Miami, he would call for Biscuit. He was sure the dog hated New York winters as much as he did. The warm south-Florida climate would be much more suitable to them both.

How had he gotten himself into this mess? He had

known Otto for years. They had served together overseas. Ironically, the killer had saved his life when an IED took out their patrol, blew their Humvee twenty feet into the air and left him without the use of one eye. Otto had survived the blast, pulled him from the wreckage, administered first aid to the wounded, and laid down protective fire until help had arrived. Otto was an interrogator, not a battle-worn soldier like the others in his unit. On the day of the attack, Otto was being transported to a black site to interrogate a high-value target reputedly responsible for the deaths of hundreds of American soldiers. But the anxiety of the ambush had proven to be too much for him. Otto shot and wounded three of his countrymen before being shot himself by retaliatory fire. Simply put, he had snapped. Later, after he had been returned stateside for evaluation, it was determined that in the moment of the attack he had suffered a complete separation from reality. He had told the doctors and nurses who treated him he was not a soldier at all but rather a famous writer and demanded to be released. They deemed him psychologically unfit for a return to duty.

Father Frank's injury had taken him out of the field and garnered him a ticket home as well. A man of the cloth, he had visited his friend in the VA hospital every day, partly because he owed him his life, but also because he was concerned about the possibility that he might strike out one day as a citizen. Otto had survived months of torture at the hands of the enemy, taken lives, and endured a horrific explosion. He had watched men die, seen bodies blown to pieces, and been so traumatically affected by it all that his body had manifested a physical reaction to stress which his doctors had diagnosed as allodynia.

On the day of his first murder, Otto confessed to his friend and asked for absolution. Father Frank accompanied him to the abandoned construction site where he observed the dead girl laying in the room. He wanted to tell Otto to surrender himself to the authorities but changed his mind. As much as his friend was now a killer, he was also a victim of his own debilitated and fragile mind. War had destroyed them both, made it impossible for them to function in modern society. There was no place for him here. He was a man caught between good and evil. It was then he decided to do the unthinkable. He would turn his back on the cross and help his friend cover up the murder. Together they cut up and disposed of the body. For reasons he did not understand, Otto insisted that the girl be covered in leaves. He talked incessantly at the time of her disposal, complimenting her on her perfect golden blonde hair, what an inspiration she had been to him, how one day he would write a wonderful story about her and that the world would know her name. He paid no attention. These were the ramblings of a man who had lost all touch with reality. He would get him the help he needed. He owed him that, but it would take time. He would have to make a case for his friend's insanity. One murder led to another, one confession to the next. Before long he found himself immersed in Otto's psychopathic world. What had started out as an intention to help his friend had resulted in his direct involvement in the crimes. Now there were too many to count. Otto was a man on a murderous rampage, intent on fulfilling a destiny which only he understood.

When they resettled in Miami, he would have a long talk with his friend, try to help him see the error of his ways and put an end to the murder spree once and for all.

A voice called out from the driver's side of the garbage truck. "Hey, pal. You like to surf?"

Father Frank recognized the code Otto had mentioned

the man would use when he made contact. "Yes," he replied. "The best waves are in Big Sur."

The man nodded. "Otto sent me," he said. "You ready to go?"

"Yeah."

The man whistled to his partner who looked over his shoulder, nodded, then resumed his surveillance of the street.

"You look familiar," Father Frank said.

"You too. The convoy, right? Iraq?"

Father Frank nodded. He recognized the soldier from the day of the attack, had even given him last rights. "Glad to see you made it back. How long have you been out of the service?"

"A while."

Frank pointed to the sign on the back of the garbage truck. "This your business?" he asked.

"Sort of. These days I mostly take care of other people's problems."

Father Frank was suddenly terror-struck. He understood what the ex-soldier meant. Before he had time to react the man had raised his weapon, touched the silencer to his forehead, and fired twice. *Thwup, thwup.*

The gunman whistled. The passenger ran back, joined him. Together they threw Father Frank's body into the bin.

The two men climbed back into the truck and drove off, leaving the dead man behind.

BACK IN THE SHANTY, lying beside Brooklyn Ben, Biscuit suddenly looked up and whined.

"What's the matter, boy?" the old man asked.

The dog let out a sorrowful cry.

## 29

BONNIE COLE MOANED in the back of the ambulance. Lacey took her hand. "It's okay, honey. We'll be there soon."

Every nerve in her body was on fire. "Must be adrenaline," Bonnie said. "I never really felt the pain until now. I guess I was putting all my energy into staying alive."

"You did that and more," Lacey said. "You helped get us out of there."

The driver's partner, paramedic Rhonda Attwell, monitored Bonnie's heart rate and blood pressure, checked her saline drip. Bonnie cried out once more. "Lace, I don't feel well."

"Can't you give her something?" Lacey asked.

Attwell shook her head. "Her wounds are septic. Given the level of infection she's presenting with we're leaving that decision up to the docs."

"But she's in so much pain."

"We're two minutes out. Soon she'll have all the help she... *dammit!*"

Bonnie's body started to shake. The paramedic leaned

forward, spoke anxiously to the driver. Suddenly the siren blared. The ambulance sped up.

"She's seizing!" Lacey yelled.

Bonnie was fully convulsive. The paramedic prepared a syringe, called out to the driver. "Tell them to have a crash team ready."

"Copy that." The driver grabbed his microphone from the console, communicated with the hospital, relayed the response. "Standing by," he replied.

The convulsions ceased. Bonnie fell back on the gurney, face slack, eyes vacant. She stared past Lacey.

"No... no... no," Lacey cried.

The paramedic yelled. "Code Blue!"

More radio chatter. "Thirty seconds to door," the driver called out, then yelled at his rig. "Come on, come on, come on!"

To Lacey, Attwell said, "Brace yourself."

Lacey grabbed the gurney side rail and steadied herself. The ambulance took a hard left, slowed, then braked to a stop.

The rear doors flew open. The crash team assisted the paramedics, pulled the gurney out of the ambulance, dropped the wheels. "Clear!" the lead doctor yelled. Attwell updated her on their patient's condition as they whisked Bonnie down the hall.

Lacey tried to stay with the team. When they reached a set of double doors that read EMERGENCY PERSONNEL ONLY BEYOND THIS POINT Attwell stopped her.

"Wait here," she said.

"But..."

Attwell paused. The paramedic placed a hand on her shoulder. "She's getting the best care now," she said. "You'll be updated as soon as we know what's going on. But I'll be frank with you. Your friend has been through a lot. Her body is in rough shape. I suggest you contact her family as soon as possible."

Lacey remembered Bonnie's husband's name: *Owen*. But she had no telephone number, no contact information, no way to reach him. The police had taken their statements outside Kessel's after learning about the women's brave escape. They would know. Her disappearance was already a matter of record. Perhaps Owen had been told his wife had been found, safe but injured, and was back at Kessel's looking for her.

The authorities would inform him that she had been transported to the hospital. They would soon be reunited.

If she were still alive when he arrived.

Lacey felt a rising panic. What if Bonnie didn't make it? What if she had come this far, only to die now? The concept of that possibility was too much to bear. The oppressive stress of the past forty-eight hours, the non-stop fearing for her life that she had refused to show to her co-captors finally caught up with her.

Back to the wall, racked with a need to release the pent-up emotion, Lacey slid to the floor, drew her knees to her chest, and sobbed.

A moment later, she heard a familiar voice. "Lace?"

Lacey looked up, wiped away her tears, caught her breath.

The big man from the Odyssey stood in front her.

"Anton," she said. She held out her arms.

Anton leaned forward and helped her to her feet. He kissed her forehead, held her close. "Thank God you're okay," he said.

"What are you doing here?" Lacey asked.

"What do you think?" Anton replied. "It's a nice day for a

drive. I had nothing better to do, so I thought I would cruise the local hospitals, maybe pick up a hot chick. You?"

Wrapped in Anton's powerful arms she felt the tension begin to leave her body. Lacey half-cried, half-laughed. It felt good. She pointed to the double doors. "I have a friend in there who's fighting for her life," she said.

"I know."

Lacey had been so focused on Anton she had not noticed the man in the dark blue jacket accompanying him. "Ms. Chastain, my name is Detective Rick Pallister, NYPD. I need to ask you a few questions. May we chat for a minute?"

Lacey looked up at Anton. "Stay with me?"

Anton looked down at her. "I'm not going anywhere."

Lacey smiled. She turned to the policeman. "Of course," she said. "I'll tell you everything you want to know."

OUTSIDE THE HOSPITAL ENTRANCE, a taxicab slowed to a stop.

"Wait here," Otto said as he opened the door.

"Not a chance," the cabbie replied. "You want me to wait, you pay in advance."

Otto fished five twenties out of his pocket and tossed them onto the back seat. "Will that do?"

"For now," the driver replied. "Half an hour, then I'm gone."

"I won't need that long," Otto replied. "Stay put. Don't make me come looking for you."

"Thirty minutes," the driver said. "Not a second longer."

Otto slammed the cab door shut and walked through the automatic doors into the Emergency Room.

## 30

JORDAN, CHRIS AND Agent Penner met Detective Rick Pallister in the Emergency lounge at Bellevue Hospital.

"What do we know?" Penner asked. "Is she alive?"

"She's hanging on," Pallister replied. "By how much I don't know. The docs are keeping pretty tight-lipped about her condition."

"Keon said there were three other survivors."

Pallister nodded. "Two are still at the scene... Kessel's Bookbinding and Restoration. You wouldn't believe the basement in that place."

The detective glanced over his shoulder, pointed out Lacey and Anton. "The woman sitting over there is the fourth vic, Lacey Chastain."

"Who's the guy?" Penner asked.

"A friend."

"They arrived together?" Penner asked.

"Mr. Moore came with me. He's been looking for Ms.

Chastain since she disappeared. She accompanied Mrs. Cole in the ambulance."

"Mrs. Cole?" Jordan said.

The detective nodded. "Victim number three. Her husband has been notified. He's on his way."

Penner glanced at Lacey. "She tell you anything?" he asked.

"Yeah," Pallister replied. "Four of them were held in the basement. As far as we know, Ms. Chastain was his latest victim. Looks like he picked the wrong girl. She was responsible for their escape."

"Just four?" Penner asked.

"That's what she said."

Lacey overheard their conversation. "There were others," she offered. "He'd kept them for a while."

Jordan walked over, presented her credentials, and sat beside Lacey. "Ms. Chastain, my name is Special Agent Jordan Quest. I'm with the FBI. What do you know about the other victims?"

"Just what Melinda and Victoria told me," Lacey replied. "They were the other two women he held prisoner. Kept them caged, like animals. He used Bonnie as a skin donor. Can you believe that? He kept her sedated for the sole purpose of removing layers of her skin." Lacey's body started to shake. Anton placed his arm around her.

"What can you tell me about him?" Jordan asked.

"Where do I begin?" Lacey said. "A ten out of ten on the creep scale. He was careful never to reveal himself to us. He wore a masquerade-style mask. You know the kind I mean? Black, rhinestones, feathers around the eyes, long, beaked nose. And a cape, draped around him, buttoned at the neck. Like in the opera."

"What did he say to you?"

"Not much. Threats mostly. His voice was unrecognizable."

"Why was that?"

"He didn't talk like you and me. He sounded... electronic."

"He was wearing a vocal synthesizer, disguising his voice."

"I guess so. One more thing."

"What's that?" Jordan asked.

"He didn't imprison me like the others."

"Why do you think that was?"

"I think he wanted me."

"You mean sexually?"

"Maybe, maybe not. It seemed more like he wanted my companionship."

"You were special to him."

"So it seems. But I honestly don't know why."

"Is there anything else you can think of that could be of help to us?" Jordan asked.

Lacey considered the question. "I think he knew all of us before he kidnapped us. We all seemed to have two things in common: rare books and an appreciation for the arts."

"How so?"

"I'm a dancer. I also study English lit and historical folklore in addition to my psychology major at NYU. Melinda and Victoria study in the same field. Bonnie's family are provisioners to the rare book restoration industry. And one more thing."

"What's that?"

"I think he's rich."

"What makes you say that?"

"If he's the same guy you're looking for he picked me up in a Bentley."

Anton spoke. "Lacey's right. I saw the car. He picked her up at the club. That was the last time anyone saw her until now. I saw the car again this morning. I went to Lacey's place to look for her. Someone tried to knock me out. The guy took off, but I saw the car, a Silver Bentley. A friend of mine ran the plate. It came back to Kessel's. That brought me to you guys and here with Lacey."

Anton conveniently neglected to share with Jordan the gunfire that had taken place at the apartment and how he believed he had shot and wounded his attacker.

"He gassed me, knocked me out," Lacey said. "He handed me a present. It was a mask, like the one he wore in the dungeon. The box started to smoke. Next thing I knew I was out cold, then restrained."

Jordan thought of the other victims and the lab reports within their case files. All the reports indicated the presence of sevoflurane, isoflurane, ether, halothane, and Fentanyl in their bloodstream; components of the knockout gas used to subdue Lacey. The woman was lucky to be alive. The potent mixture had proven deadly to Scroll's previous victims.

"Do you think you would recognize him if you saw him again?" Jordan asked.

Lacey shook her head. "I wish I could say yes, but he disguised himself completely." Lacey stood. "This is too much for me right now. I need a minute for myself. Do you mind?"

"Not at all, Ms. Chastain," Jordan said. "Take all the time you need."

"Thank you. I need to go for a walk, get my head straight."

"I'll go with you," Anton said.

Lacey shook her head. "That's okay. I'm fine. I just need a little time on my own to think."

"You sure?" Anton said.

"Positive."

"Okay. I'll be right here when you get back."

Lacey stroked the side of his face. "I know you will, sweetie. Thank you."

LACEY WALKED down the corridor and turned the corner. The reader board adjacent to the elevator indicated the cafeteria was located on the second floor. A cup of hot coffee would be perfect, she thought. She pressed the call button, waited for the elevator to arrive, stepped inside. The doors began to close.

A voice called out. "Hold the door!"

Lacey pressed the OPEN button on the panel and waited for the doors to open.

"Thank you," the man said as he backed a wheelchair into the small elevator.

"You're welcome," Lacey replied. She watched the doors close. "What floor?"

The man turned and covered his mouth and nose. "Hello, Lacey," he said. "Did you miss me?"

Otto shoved the small canister in her face and pulled the trigger. Lacey breathed in the gas. Immediately she fell forward into his arms, unconscious.

Otto eased her into the wheelchair and redirected the elevator to the first floor.

Together they exited the hospital. The driver had waited.

The cabbie looked puzzled. "She okay?" he asked.

Otto opened the back door and eased Lacey into the seat. "Fine," he said. "My sister. Colonoscopy. She never could handle the sedative. She's still pretty out of it. Do me a favor and pop the trunk."

The driver nodded. "I can't handle anesthesia either," he said. "Takes me forever to come around. Where to?"

Otto folded the wheelchair and placed it in the trunk of the cab. "Home," he replied. "Take us home."

# 31

HOMICIDE DETECTIVE DAVID Keon stood over The Wolf's body as members of the forensics team photographed the scene, dusted the bathroom for fingerprints, swabbed her body for evidence and removed the balloon bags of cocaine from her stomach cavity.

Crime Scene Investigator Evan Mallory spoke as he watched his team work. "We should just leave her to rot. Let the rats have her."

Keon examined the evidence bag that held the latest scroll intended for Commissioner Haley. "No argument here," the detective replied. "What problem do you suppose Scroll had with a low-life drug dealer like Rosalita Sanchez?"

"Beat's me," Mallory said. "But I've got no problem with him taking out the trash."

Keon's phone rang. He checked the display. Pallister was calling. He stepped out of the room and picked up. "Tell me you're having a better day than I am," he said.

Pallister replied. “Maybe. I’m at Bellevue with Lacey Chastain and our friends from the Bureau.”

“How is she doing?”

“As well as can be expected.”

“And the other vic? Bonnie Cole?”

“Don’t know yet. She coded on the way in. Girl’s in rough shape.”

“Fucking bastard.”

“Tell me about it.”

“Scroll hit again. I’m at the scene. He took out The Wolf.”

“Rosalita Sanchez? Did he leave a scroll?”

“Yeah. But you’ll never believe this.”

“What?”

“He says he did it to save the lives of her kids. And I quote: ‘The children are innocent. The woman is not. This is the start. There will be more.’”

“Nice to know we’re dealing with a compassionate psychopath.”

“You want me to head over to Bellevue?”

“Yeah. And bring the scroll. Perhaps Agent Quest can tell us more if she reads it.”

“By reading you mean doing her psychic mumbo-jumbo thing?”

“Yeah,” Pallister replied. “But I’ve gotta say, my opinion of the woman is changing.”

“How’s that?”

“Penner told me she zeroed in on the Cassidy Valentine crime scene like nothing he’d ever seen before. Took them straight to ground zero.”

“You believe the guy?”

“I might think he’s an asshole, but he’s got no reason to lie about that.”

"That's high praise coming from you."

"He said if he hadn't experienced it personally, he'd never have believed it."

"Good enough," Keon agreed. "We've got nothing to lose. I'm willing to give her the benefit of the doubt. I'll wrap up here and be on my way. Give me thirty."

"Later," Pallister replied. He hung up.

---

THE MOOD in the Emergency waiting room was somber as the team waited for an update on the status of Bonnie Cole. Special Agent Penner spoke to Chris. "You two been working together for a while?"

Chris shook his head. "Just since Jordan graduated from Quantico."

Penner scoffed. "They paired you with a rookie? Jesus, who'd you piss off?"

Chris let the comment go. It would be just like Penner to make an uninformed and pompous remark. Instead, he answered, "The Director himself partnered us."

"Dunn set you up?"

Chris nodded. "You've never heard the story?"

Penner shook his head.

"It happened three years ago," Chris said, "Someone had kidnapped the Director's daughters. Jordan was instrumental in saving their lives. She wasn't with the Bureau then. He had learned of her abilities and sought her out. There is no doubt in my mind that if it had not been for her Director Dunn would have lost his girls. We worked together on that case, which also came with a great personal loss to Jordan. A lesser woman would have folded under the pressure, but not Jordan. She made it through and came out the other side, stronger than before. That rookie you're talking about is already a legend in the Bureau. Which leaves me with just one question."

"What's that?" Penner asked.

Chris stood and stared down Penner. "While that rookie's been busy making bureau history, what the hell have you been doing?"

Chris left the senior agent to think about his words and walked over to Jordan. "How are you doing?"

"I'm not sure," Jordan replied.

"What do you mean?"

"Something's off."

"I know that tone," Chris said. "What's up?"

"Have you seen Ms. Chastain?"

"Not since she went for a walk. Why?"

"Something's wrong. I can feel it." Jordan called out to Agent Penner. "Search the hospital. Now."

"What's wrong?" Anton said.

"I think Lacey is missing," Jordan said.

Anton overheard, ran down the corridor, looked around the corner, ran back. "I don't see her."

"I'll check the cafeteria," Penner said.

"Jordan and I will sweep the even floors. Anton, Detective Pallister, you take the odd."

"You got it," Pallister said. "I'll contact security and have them station a guard here. If Lacey returns, I'll have them call me. Then I'll call you."

"Go!" Chris said.

The teams ran off in search of the young woman. Jordan reached the elevator and stopped. She turned to Chris. "She's not here."

"We have to check."

"There's no point." She placed her palm over the lift's keypad. "Scroll was here."

"Are you telling me he came here looking for her?"

"That's exactly what I'm saying. He has her. Again."

"Then forget checking the floors," Chris said as he headed for the stairs. "We need to look at the security footage. No one knows what Scroll looks like. We find Lacey on camera and we find our guy. As soon as we know who we're looking for it's over. Scroll is ours."

Jordan followed. "And Lacey is safe," she replied.

"Assuming he hasn't harmed her."

"I'm not getting that. Just a lot of anger."

"What about a timeline? How far ahead of us is he?"

"Ten minutes. Fifteen maybe."

"We can work with that."

The agents broke through the basement doors. A sign on the wall, Security Services, indicated that the office was down the corridor. Chris and Jordan ran inside, flashed their credentials. "FBI," Chris told the officer seated at the reception desk. "I need to see the footage for all floors going back fifteen minutes. Put it up, now!"

"Yes, sir," the guard replied.

The twelve screens, one for each floor, came alive.

"Speed up the replay," Chris said. "Hurry!"

The officer turned the master control knob. Fast motion images flickered across each of the screens.

"There!" Jordan said.

Lacey Chastain, chin resting on her chest, unconscious and seated in a wheelchair, was being wheeled out of the hospital by an unknown man.

Chris pointed to the screen. "Freeze it!"

The security officer stopped the footage, then advanced it slowly. The agents watched as Scroll eased Lacey into the back seat of a Yellow taxicab, then hopped into the car himself. Slowly, the taxi pulled away from its stand.

For the first time since the investigation began, the agents got their first grainy glimpse of the man the media had dubbed The Scroll Killer.

"Gotcha, you sonofabitch!" Chris said.

## 32

OTTO WAS PLEASED with the progress he had made over the last three years. His book of stories had grown to thirty-three. He hoped his late mother, Eva Schreiber-Kessel, would be pleased.

Eva had come from literary royalty. Her great grandfather had been Jacob Grimm of the famed Brothers Grimm, authors of Grimm's Fairy Tales. She spoke of him often when Otto was a child and impressed upon him that someday he too would grow up to be a great writer, just like his great-great-grandfather. It was, as she said, in the genes.

However, it soon became clear the wondrous storytelling abilities possessed by his celebrated descendent had skipped a generation. No matter how hard he tried, Otto lacked the fertile imagination required to succeed as a storyteller. As a teen he would sit for hours, pondering and structuring his stories. But every word he penned met with criticism. He could still hear his mother's words in his head after reading one of his tales. *Your story has no depth, Otto... The setting is all wrong... Your characters are not believable.* At every turn she found fault with his work. *Why can't you write like your great-great- grandfather? It's in you, Otto*, she would say. *Work harder. Find it. Think, Otto! Do you know what your problem is? You have no life experience. You haven't known suffering. Your great-great-grandfather suffered, lost everything. You have it too good. You can't even live up to your family name. Do you know what Schreiber means, Otto? 'One who is engaged in literary composition; an author; a writer of novels.' That cannot be a coincidence. This is your birthright, Otto. Why can't you live up to what is yours?* With that, Eva Schreiber would leave her son to sit and think at the antique writing desk in his room; the same desk that had once belonged to his great-great-grandfather and at which were penned some of the greatest fantasy works of all time.

*You haven't known enough suffering, Otto. Make it real... make it real...*

The murders had been real enough. He had seen to that. His victim's suffering had been real enough. And what Otto lacked in imagination he made up for in ample quantity with real-life experience. He used his great-great-grandfather's stories as the foundation upon which to build his own and accomplished what he could never have done; made them *better*. By comparison, the old man's stories lacked character. Where they were born of fiction, Otto's stories were cast in fact. His story lines were *real*. The killing was *real*. The pursuit by authorities in the perfection of his craft was *real*. Unlike his famous ancestor, he did not have to endure suffering to be published. The New York Times had published every scroll he had ever submitted to them. In fact, in the age of the Internet, the stories written about him had garnered international attention. His fame *exceeded* that of his predecessor. In addition, the media had given him a pen name which he rather liked, The Scroll Killer. His great-great-grandfather had penned over two hundred stories in his lifetime. Otto had many yet to write. But he was grateful for the example he had been given. He would model his work after him, improve upon the tales he had written, as he had with Rosalita Sanchez and his great-great-grandfather's tale, The Wolf and the Seven Young Kids.

Similarly, Courtney Valentine, with her luminous golden hair, reminded him of the story of Rapunzel. He had met the beautiful young nurse while attending a recovery and transition program at the Madison Institute, a satellite clinic of the Veterans Administration Hospital on the top floor of the Beamont Building in Queens. Her perfect looks suited her fairy tale namesake, and she would blush every time he told her how beautiful she was, how she was born to fame, and that one day he would name a story after her. He did not understand why she seemed so shocked when he met her in the underground parking lot of the Beaumont, told her it was finally time to meet her destiny, and dosed her with his special spray. Some women were born to be famous. He simply facilitated the process. Perhaps in the afterlife Courtney would better understand that his intention was nothing but honorable.

His first kill, in which he slit the throat of the stewardess in Miami, was the only murder by which he had not sought to improve upon the stories of his great-great-grandfather. That woman had just been a condescending bitch who deserved to die. He had been happy to help her on her way.

The woman whose hands he had amputated and left in the trunk of her car in Bedford-Stuyvesant had belittled him when he mistook her for a high-priced call girl. She had had the nerve to tell him she'd rather sell her soul to the Devil than allow him to lay his hands on her, much less have sex with him. He saw to it she would never lay her hands on another man ever again. Which turned out to be a very short time. He gassed, bound, and gagged her, forced her into the trunk of the car and cut off her hands with the army knife he kept strapped to his leg. When she had bled out to his satisfaction, he closed the trunk and left her to die. His great-great-grandfather's story, The Girl with No Hands, had been his inspiration for her murder.

So many stories had been written and so many more were left to write. Leaving the scrolls behind at the murder scenes differentiated his work from that of his famous relative. The media liked it too. It had become his brand.

*You haven't known enough suffering, Otto. Make it real... make it real...*

He would make it real, all right. And then some.

By the time he was done killing he would be more famous than his great-great-grandfather ever was.

His stories, too, would live on.

Infamy was much more appealing than fame.

"You sure she's okay?"

The words shook Otto out of his daydream, brought him back to reality.

"What's that?" he asked the cab driver.

"Your sister. She's out cold. Maybe she should have stayed in the hospital a little longer. Taken more time to recover."

"She'll be fine."

The cabbie shrugged. "If you say so."

"I know so."

"So where's home?"

"What do you mean?"

"You told me to drive you home. But you didn't say where home was."

"Across the bridge," Otto replied. "Brooklyn Heights. Joralemon and Hicks. Conroy Apartments."

The cabbie nodded. "I know it."

Lacey stirred, then fell back to sleep.

He had written so many stories. So many more were left to write.

He remembered his mother's words: *Make it real, Otto... make it real.*

He would make it real. And, in doing so, make it right.

# 33

CHRIS AND JORDAN called Special Agent Penner and Detective Pallister and instructed them to meet them in the hospital security office. Anton arrived with the homicide detective.

Chris pointed to the still capture on the monitor. "That's him," he said. "That's Scroll."

Pallister turned to Anton. "Is that the same guy who attacked you?"

"I think so," Anton replied.

"What do you mean?" Penner quipped. "Either he is, or he isn't."

"Back off, Penner," Pallister said. "Mr. Moore is a witness, not a suspect."

"I only saw the side of his face for a few seconds," Anton said. "He had his back to me the whole time. But the clothing's the same."

"Hell of a lot of good that does us," Penner said.

Anton dismissed the agent's remark. "What about Lacey?" he asked. "Is she all right?"

To the security officer Chris said, "Roll it back." The

officer turned back the recording by five seconds. The footage revealed an unconscious Lacey slumped in a wheelchair."

Anton clasped his hands behind his head. "He's got her! Oh, Jesus!"

Penner barked at the security officer. "Can you get us a better angle?"

The officer pressed several buttons on the control panel. "Watch monitor number four," he said. The picture advanced slowly.

"Stop!" Penner said. "Now move it ahead, frame-by-frame."

As Otto Schreiber leaned forward to help Lacey out of the wheelchair, he glanced up at the security camera in the Emergency entrance portico. The picture was opaque, blurred.

"Can you sharpen the image?" Penner asked.

The officer shook his head. "It's not me," he replied. "It's the camera. There's dirt on the lens cover. That's the best I can do."

"Give me a printout," Penner demanded.

The guard walked to the computer printer and waited for the machine to come online. "One second," he said.

Anton was devastated. "This would never have happened if I'd gone with her for that walk," he said. "No way he would have gotten past me. Not a second time."

"No one saw this coming, Anton," Jordan said. "You're not to blame. We let our guard down."

Chris and Penner walked over, interrupted. "We have a problem," Chris said, holding up the printout. "Picture's no good. We can't put it over the air. No one would recognize Scroll from this."

"What about the taxi number?" Jordan asked.

"Same deal," Chris replied. "Can't make it out."

"You mean only one camera captured a picture of the cab?" Jordan asked.

"That specific location is a dead zone," the security officer stated. "Our entire system is being upgraded. That's the only camera we have that's operational in that area right now."

"Perfect," Penner said. "We have the guy in our grasp, but we don't know what the hell he looks like or how to find him."

"Yes, we do," Pallister offered.

"How's that?" Penner asked.

"Dash cams." The detective said. "We need to review the footage again. We might not be able to make out the cab number, but we know where it was parked. The time stamp on the video will tell us when it was there. Only a few cabs made pick-ups or drop-offs in the last fifteen minutes. We need to contact those cab companies. Find out which of their vehicles were there at that time. Most fleet cabs are equipped with front- and rearview security cameras with hard drives that record continuously in the event of an accident. We can check their footage, find out which one caught the number of Scroll's cab, put out a BOLO and find that vehicle. HRT will execute a hard target takedown on the car. We can end this today."

"I'll make the calls and put the Hostage Rescue Team on standby," Penner said.

Jordan turned to Anton. "We'll get her back," she said.

Anton didn't reply. He sat in silence and stared at the foggy image of Scroll on the computer screen. The agent's confidence did nothing to allay his fear of losing the woman he loved, perhaps for the last time.

Anton stood, turned to Pallister. “We need to leave,” he said. “Go after him.”

“I’m sorry, Mr. Moore,” the detective apologized. “This is police business now. For your safety I can’t have you traveling with me any longer. You’ll need to make alternate arrangements to get back home.”

Anton nodded. “I understand,” he replied.

The detective shook the big man’s hand. “I promise you the minute we locate Ms. Chastain I’ll be in touch.”

“Thank you, Detective. I’d appreciate that.”

“Take care of yourself.”

“I will.”

Pallister rejoined his colleagues at the computer station.

Anton made a call.

Mike Degario looked at the call display, picked up right away. “‘Bout friggin’ time you got back to me.”

“Sorry, Mike.”

“Did you find Lacey?”

“Yes. But there’s been a complication.”

“What kind of complication?”

“I don’t have time to get into the details right now,” Anton replied. “You think Russ’ offer is still on the table? Can we use his guys?”

“You kidding? My phone’s been burning up. Word’s out about Lacey. Everyone’s worried sick. What do you need?”

“Lacey left here around twenty minutes ago in a cab.”

“Have the cops track the cab number and find her. No big deal.”

“It’s a long story, but that’s not possible.”

“What about running the license plate?”

“Don’t know it.”

Frustrated, Mike said. “Okay, what *do* you know?”

"Only that she left here unconscious in the back seat of a cab with a guy the cops think might be The Scroll Killer."

"Holy shit!"

"We need feet on the street, Mike. Guys who'll force every fucking cab off the road if they have to to find Lacey and not be afraid to put a boot up the ass of any sonofabitch who puts up a fight. You know the type I'm talking about."

"Hells Angels... Outlaws... Forbidden Ones. Shall I continue?"

"Exactly. Tell Russ to contact the chapter president of every biker gang he knows. They're regulars at the Odyssey. All their guys know Lacey. She's like a little sister to them. Tell Russ to put the word out. They need to start looking for her."

"You've got it."

"And one more thing."

"What's that?"

"I need a favor."

Mike chuckled. "Of course, you do. You still at the hospital?"

"Yeah."

"I'm on my way."

"Thanks, buddy."

"Hang in there, Anton. We're going to get her back. Trust me, the guy that took her is street meat."

"Tell Russ to relay a message to the guys from me, will ya?" Anton said.

"What's that?"

"When they find him take him somewhere special and hold him for me. He's mine."

"With pleasure," Mike replied.

## 34

THE CAB PULLED up to the Conroy Apartments in Brooklyn Heights. Lacey was still asleep, her head laying on Otto's shoulder.

The driver turned in his seat and whispered. "You want a hand getting her inside?"

"That would be wonderful," Otto replied. "Thank you."

"No trouble."

The cabbie removed the stolen wheelchair from the trunk of the taxi. Otto opened the door, eased Lacey into his arms, then slid her into the chair.

"Thank you for all your help," Otto said.

The cabbie smiled. "My pleasure," he said. He turned to leave.

"Would I be able to ask one small favor before you go?" Otto said.

The driver checked his watch. "I have another fare," he said. "I need to be on my way."

"My apartment is at the back of the building," Otto said. "There's a three-step walk up. Problem is the entrance isn't wheelchair accessible. Can you give me a hand lifting the chair up the steps? We'll be good to go from there."

"I'm sorry," the cabbie said. "I'm really pressed for time."

"Please, I only need two more minutes of your time." Otto removed twenty dollars from his pocket and held it out to the driver. "It's extra money, off the books."

The driver looked at Lacey, felt bad for her. The poor woman needed to get inside, lay down, sleep, recover.

"I can help you inside with the chair but then I have to go," the cabbie said.

"Thank you so much," Otto said. "I'll be sure to tell my sister how helpful you were."

The driver smiled. "Around the back?"

Otto nodded. "Apartment 1C."

The cabbie walked with him as they circled the building. He helped Otto lift the wheelchair up the three steps to the side door. "If you can just grab the door and lift the front of the chair," Otto said, "I'll push her through."

Back to the door, the cabbie turned the knob, opened the door, and eased the wheelchair into the small entranceway. On the landing, he was presented with two flights of stairs. The set on his left led downstairs. The second, behind him, led up to the main floor. He looked around. "I don't see the entrance to apartment 1–"

Otto rammed the wheelchair into the man's legs. The taxi driver buckled over, cried out in pain, lost both his footing and grip on the wheelchair. A second assault sent him tumbling head over heels to the bottom of the concrete stairs.

Otto pushed the chair aside and followed the man down as he fell. Before the taxi driver had stopped rolling, Otto had removed his knife from its leg sheath and plunged it deep into the man's back once, twice, three times. The man made no noise. His eyes were open, his stare vacant. His head lay at a grotesque angle. He had broken his neck in the fall.

Using the knife had been unnecessary.

Oh, well.

Otto moved the cabbie's dead body along the hallway to the supply closet, fumbled for the key on his keychain, unlocked the door, then dumped the corpse unceremoniously into the room.

No one would look for the man in here. Otto owned this building and nine others like it, including Kessel's. Coming from a wealthy family and inheriting his mother's estate on her death had its perks.

Otto rifled through the cabbie's pocket, fished out his car keys, then closed and locked the supply room door. He needed to get rid of the cab as soon as possible.

With Lacey fast asleep in the wheelchair, Otto stepped outside, walked casually to the taxicab, drove the vehicle to the back of the apartment and parked it in the visitor's lot.

Two spaces down sat his second car, a silver Range Rover. He opened the door, hopped into the driver's seat, started the car, and drove to the side of the building where the cab had been parked.

Otto eased the wheelchair back down steps, rolled Lacey to the vehicle and opened the rear door. He lifted her out of the chair and gently moved her into the back seat. From the glove box he removed two nylon zip-ties, bound her feet and hands, and buckled her into the car. He placed the wheelchair in the rear hatch. Though there would likely be no further use for the device it could prove useful if Lacey needed to be restrained in the future.

Otto thought about the killings. He had mastered the art of murder, evaded capture by the authorities, and used his experiences to pen stories that rivaled if not exceeded the works of his great-great-grandfather.

Perhaps the time to retire from killing had arrived. With Lacey now in his life, he had everything he ever wanted. He was wealthy, young, privileged and internationally famous. She was magnificent, intelligent, and well-educated. Together they shared an appreciation for the arts. Over time, she would forgive him for the forceful manner by which he had brought them together.

He stared at the girl.

So beautiful.

His mother would have approved.

Otto pushed the START button on the Range Rover. In three hours, they would start a new life together at sea on his motor yacht. He put the car into gear and began their journey to Montauk. It was a perfect day for a drive.

THE CAB COMPANY dispatcher tried to reach the driver for the third time. "8C82 respond."

No reply.

"8C82... call in please."

The dispatcher waited. Dead air.

"8C82..."

Mary Reed knew the driver. Manny Manchescu was a reliable employee, a veteran of the industry. It was not like him to disregard a call.

Mary picked up the phone and called her supervisor. Her words made her feel uneasy. She dared not think about the possibilities.

"Sir, I think 8C82 is in trouble," she reported.

## 35

SHANE "BLADE" WATSON sat across the table from his rivals. The New York City Hells Angels chapter president made his position clear. "This meeting doesn't change a thing. I'm here for Russ and Lacey, not for you two. We find her and the piece of shit that took her. After that, it's business as usual. You stay the fuck out of our way, and we'll stay the fuck out of yours. Understood?"

"Calm down, Blade," Russ Paley said. The tension in the Odyssey Gentlemen's Club owner's office was palpable. "I didn't ask you here to broker a peace treaty. I want my girl back, plain and simple. And you guys can make that happen faster than the cops ever could."

Ray Newman, chapter president for the Outlaws motorcycle club, spoke next. "I'll put my guys on notice." To Blade he said. "You don't have to worry about starting a war. Lacey's a civilian. We're here to help."

"Agreed," Don Morris said. "Forbidden Ones will stand together on this." The chapter president extended his hand to his fellow bike gang leaders. "For Lacey?" he proposed.

The men shook hands. "For Lacey," they agreed.

To Paley, Blade said, "Tell us what you need, Russ."

Russ Paley handed the men a promotional picture of the young dancer. "Get out your phones. Take a shot of Lacey and get her picture out to your people. Get them patrolling the streets. Look everywhere. Anton wanted you to know the FBI and NYPD are looking for her too. The guy who has her is the suspected Scroll Killer. If that's true Lacey's life is in jeopardy. Forget days. She's got hours, maybe less. Who knows what this sick sonofabitch has planned for her."

"Where's Anton now?" Ray Newman asked.

"Degario's picking him up from Bellevue. Mike said Lacey was last seen being wheeled out of the hospital in a Yellow cab with the guy the cops are looking for. She was unconscious."

"He hurt her?" Blade asked.

"We don't know," Russ replied.

"Probably used formaldehyde or an injectable to knock her out," Newman suggested.

"He must have," Don Morris agreed. "Lacey strikes me as a fighter. No way she'd go with him willingly. How's Anton holding up?"

"Not so good," Russ replied. "He's worried sick."

Blade's phone chimed. He confirmed the text. "Lacey's picture's been broadcast to the club," he reported. He stood. "We need to be on the street. We're wasting time sitting around here."

Newman and Morris rose. "I suggest we divide up the city, work it by sector," Newman suggested. "My guys will take downtown and Manhattan to the Hudson. Staten Island and the harbor too."

"We'll take everything north of Manhattan," Morris said.

"Fair enough," Blade said. "I've put everybody on the road. We'll take east of the city. I'll call New Jersey, get their chapter involved too. No way she's slipping through the cracks."

"Thanks, boys," Russ said.

"You said it was a Yellow Cab?" Newman asked.

"Yes," Russ replied. "Why?"

"One of my guys is a mechanic. Works in their fleet service department."

"Think he can find out what cab picked up the call at Bellevue?"

Newman took out his phone as he left the office. "I'll ask."

"Ballsy move taking a cab," Blade said.

"Yeah," Morris agreed. "Not the brightest idea. Probably thought he could hide in plain sight."

"So far it's working," Blade said.

"What if Lacey wakes up?" Morris asked. "It's over then. She'll try to escape. He'll kill her and the driver."

"Not if he keeps her sedated," Blade said.

Newman returned to the room. "We may have something. My guy says everything's going fucking crazy at Yellow. Cops have been all over the place asking questions. One of their hacks is missing."

"Did he say when they lost track of the cab?" Morris asked.

"There's been no radio contact for the last half-hour."

"Maybe he's on his lunch break," Blade said.

Newman shook his head. "The cars GPS last placed it in Brooklyn Heights at the Conroy Apartments. That was also the driver's last reported drop-off."

"I'm sending my guys there now," Blade said. He placed a call. "Maybe we can beat the cops to Lacey."

# 36

AGENT PENNER ENDED the call. "That was the Bureau," he said. "Both Boro and Yellow had cabs running calls to and from the hospital at the time of Ms. Chastain's abduction." He smirked at Detective Pallister. "You were right about the dash cams. A Boro cab caught a video of Scroll putting Lacey in the backseat of a Yellow cab. Number is 8C82. They called the company to speak with the driver. Can't raise him on the radio. They have his last location before he went dark: Conroy Apartments in Brooklyn Heights. I've called Keon and asked him to meet us there. This is the closest we've come to nailing down a location for Scroll. We need to move on this, fast."

The agents thanked the security officer and left the office.

"Keon says Scroll hit again," Detective Pallister shared the news with the team as they left the hospital. "Some drug dealer named Rosalita Sanchez. Eviscerated her. But get this. He called it in this time."

"He identified himself?" Chris asked.

Pallister shook his head. "Not exactly. Dave said the

Commissioner's office received an anonymous call from Sanchez's cellphone. No one on the line. 9-1-1 dispatched officers to the scene figuring the caller might be unconscious. They called the task force when they found her."

"Did he leave a note?" Jordan asked.

"Yeah. Said she wasn't the first and won't be the last, and that her kids are innocent. This guy brutally murders Sanchez, then shows concern for the welfare of her children. Can you believe that?"

THE CONROY APARTMENTS was a full-fledged crime scene. The team arrived to find the decedent, Manny Manchescu, the cab driver, in the care of the Office of the Coroner. Detective Dave Keon provided an update as they crossed under the black and yellow barrier tape that kept onlookers at bay.

"We found him downstairs in the supply room," Keon reported. "Blood was seeping out from under the door. Three stab wounds to the lower back and a broken neck. That's one lousy way to check out."

"Let me guess," Penner said. "No witnesses."

"One, but not too credible." Keon pointed to a kindly looking old lady standing in her pink track suit beside her dog. "That's Mrs. Sheen. The lab is Taffy. Mrs. Sheen says she saw the cab arrive. The driver helped a man push a woman in a wheelchair into the building around the back."

"She give you a description of Scroll?"

"*Scroll?*" Keon asked.

"That's who we figure killed the cab driver and kidnapped the woman."

"Jesus."

"What's the deal with Mrs. Sheen?" Chris asked.

"I don't think she's altogether there. I asked her if she could provide me with a description of the man she saw. She put him in his mid-to-late thirties, about five-foot-ten, medium build, with brown hair and a kind face."

"Sounds like a pretty good description to me," Penner said.

"And a dead ringer for Tom Cruise. Apparently, so am I. And the Coroner. And just about every other cop on the scene."

"That kind of changes things."

"Just a tad."

"Maybe you'll get a more accurate statement from the dog," Chris joked.

"There was one thing Mrs. Sheen said that *was* significant," Keon said.

"What's that?" Penner asked.

"Our guy arrived in the cab, but he left in a silver Range Rover. She remembers part of the license plate: MRG..."

"Where's the cab?" Pallister asked.

Jordan had walked away from the team, headed toward the back of the building. She called out. "Here, around back. Visitors parking lot."

The team joined her at the vehicle.

Penner theorized the sequence of events. "So, he brings Lacey here by cab on the premise of... what? Taking her back to his place? He couldn't be that stupid."

"He wasn't," Jordan said. She opened the car door. "He needed to switch cars. Probably figured that his image had been captured on the security camera at the hospital. The cab ride was a means to an end. The driver was collateral damage." She pointed to the brake and accelerator pedals. "Look. Blood."

"Other than the scrolls," Chris said, "that's the first real piece of evidence we've found so far."

"Speaking of scrolls," Keon said. He removed the evidence from his pocket and handed it to Jordan. "This one was found on Rosalita Sanchez's body. I thought you might want to examine it."

Jordan took the scroll. She shared the details of the crime scene with the team as they flashed through her mind. Rosalita being surprised in her bathroom... the killers knife dragging across her throat, then cutting deep into her stomach, gutting her... filling her with drugs.

"How could you possibly know that?" Keon said in amazement. "Astounding."

Jordan then revealed something unique about the vision which ventured beyond the examination of the physical evidence. "He's talking to himself while he's killing her," she said. "Rambling on. Muttering something under his breath. Make it real... something... Make it real... *Otto*? Yes, a name: Otto."

Penner speculated. "What if the only thing that's off about Mrs. Sheen's observation is this guy's resemblance to Tom Cruise? What if everything else is correct? What if we have our description? Five-foot-ten, brown hair, medium build, mid-to-late thirties, good-looking, first name Otto. We need to pull out all the stops. Rick, run the info through the DMV and see if we get a hit. Dave, take the Boro cab dash cam photo and our pic from the hospital, grainy as it is, and have the uniforms start a door-to-door in this building and the shops around Kessel's Restoration. See if someone confirms the name Otto against the picture. Jordan, Chris, and I will talk to the Coroner. See if there's anything more he can tell us about the drivers murder."

"You got it," Pallister said.

"On it," Keon replied.

The men left to complete their assignments.

To Penner and Chris, Jordan said. "There was one more thing I kept seeing. But I have no idea what it means."

"What's that?" Chris asked.

"A word. Montauk."

# 37

THE SILVER RANGE ROVER left Brooklyn Heights and traveled east along Interstate 495 toward Montauk. Laying in the backseat, hands and feet now bound by plastic zip ties, upper body and legs held tightly in place by the seat restraints, Lacey drifted in and out of consciousness as the effect of the knock-out gas subsided. The smell of the leather seat cushion upon which she lay stirred her senses. She clung to the aroma, focused on it, breathed it in, shallow inhalations at first, then deeper, used it as a sensory anchor until at last she came around, opened her eyes, and became aware of the bindings that trapped her as tightly as a rabbit in a snare.

Lacey struggled to free herself. Impossible. She recognized her surroundings -the back seat of a car- and panicked. Someone spoke from the front seat.

"Good afternoon, sunshine," the voice said. "Sleep well?"

No, Lacey thought. It couldn't be. Her head ached; her body felt numb. She knew the feeling, had experienced it before while recovering from the incapacitating gas from the gift box presented to her by the driver of the Bentley at the club. "You," she said.

"My name is Otto," the man replied. "It's wonderful to speak with you again, Lacey. I hope you're not too uncomfortable. I'll let you stretch your legs as soon as we arrive at our destination. Shouldn't be more than a few hours from now. Sound good?"

"Fuck you."

Otto dynamited the brake pedal, tapped it hard, then hit the gas. The sudden lurching motion threw Lacey forward in her seat, then back. Instinctively, she tried to brace herself. The plastic zip ties through which the seat restraints had been passed cinched tightly around her hands and feet and cut off her circulation. The sudden pain in her extremities felt as if they had been severed from her body.

"Unpleasantness like that won't be tolerated," Otto said. "You're far too beautiful to possess such a filthy mouth."

"What do you want from me?" Lacey asked.

"The remainder of your days," Otto replied.

"What is that supposed to mean?"

Otto paused. "Do you believe in love at first sight, Lacey?"

Lacey said nothing. She tried to lift her hands, to get to the zip tie that bound her wrists. The seat restraint immobilized her arms.

Otto continued. "I do. From the moment I saw you dancing at the Odyssey I knew you were the one for me. We're meant to be together."

Lacey recognized the obsessive sound in his voice. She'd dealt with men like this in the past. Men who had fallen in love with her hard and fast. As much as her beauty had provided her with many wonderful opportunities in life it had also been a curse. She had found herself in precarious situations before but nothing as demented and unpredictable as this. She was out of her depth with this man and at a disadvantage. There was only one way to deal with this situation. She would need to give in to him, buy time and trust he wouldn't kill her. She would need to push him emotionally, make him fall even harder for her. Then, when the time was right, she would do whatever it took to survive.

"Now I recognize you," Lacey lied. She softened the tone of her voice. "Yes, from the club. Why didn't you tell me it was you?"

Otto tried to control his rising anger. "Don't patronize me, Lacey. You looked right past me while I sat there, watching you, dreaming about you. You never even gave me a second glance."

"Oh, Otto," Lacey replied. The vocal inflection was mellifluous now, purposefully sultry. "I'm sorry if I gave you that impression. That wasn't the case at all. It's the lighting in the club, the strobes and spotlights. I can't see the audience from the stage. All I see is white light. Why didn't you come visit me after my show? We could have spent time together, gotten to know one another. That would have been perfectly fine with me."

"It would?" Otto asked.

"Of course," Lacey urged. "There's nothing to say we can't make up for lost time. Would that be all right? If we spent time together now?"

Otto was perplexed. The most beautiful girl in his world was in his back seat and *wanted* him. His plan had changed. Perhaps he would not have to torture her into submission after all.

"They hurt, Otto," Lacey said.

"What hurts?"

Lacey tried to raise her wrists. Otto glanced at her in the

rearview mirror. "The plastic ties. They're cutting into my skin."

"You can wait a while longer."

"I can't feel my hands."

"We'll be in Montauk soon. I'll cut you free then."

"What if that's too late," Lacey asked. "You don't want me to lose the use of my hands, do you?"

"No."

"Then cut me loose, please. Let me sit up front with you. You'd prefer that, wouldn't you?"

"You'll try to escape."

"No, Otto," Lacey replied. "I'd never leave you. Why would I want to do that? Everything I need is right here with you. But it can't be like this. Not bound in the back seat like an animal. Cut me loose. Let me be the Lacey you want me to be."

God, she was beautiful. He wanted so badly to believe her.

"I want to trust you," Otto said.

"As you should."

Otto conceded. "All right," he said. "At the next exit. You can sit up front with me."

"Thank you."

"You're welcome."

"You're a good man, Otto."

"I'm trying."

# 38

MIKE DEGARIO'S PHONE rang. He took the call, listened. "Got it," he said. "Thanks."

"Who was that?" Anton asked.

"Russ Paley. Everyone's on board. Angels, Outlaws, Forbidden Ones. They've got Lacey's picture. They're on the street looking for her now."

"Where?"

"Everywhere. New York's blanketed."

"What if he's already taken her out of state?"

"Angels have Jersey covered. I would imagine Connecticut, too. But he couldn't have that big of a lead on us, could he?"

"I don't think so," Anton replied.

"Then why worry about it? Don't borrow trouble, Anton. We have enough to deal with as it is."

"You're right."

"I'm always right. So where to?"

"That's the problem. I'm not sure. We can't just drive around the city without a plan."

"You're a personal security specialist," Degario said. "What would you do if Lacey was your client, and you thought her life was in peril?"

"Leave the city. I would want to put as much distance between us and the danger as possible. I'd go somewhere no one knew us, assess the situation with a clear head, figure things out."

"How would you get to where you wanted to go the fastest?"

"I'd take the Interstate. Head east."

"Why?"

"I'd want to go to the countryside. There are fewer people there, less likelihood they'd pay attention to us. We would be just another couple of tourists to them. Then maybe find a summer home we could break in to where we could hold up for a while."

"Sounds like a sound plan," Mike said.

"Yeah, except it's all speculation. We can't count on any of it."

"I'm not so sure," Mike argued. "If I'm wanted by the cops and I've got a bullet in my shoulder *and* I'm in the company of someone I've kidnapped that sounds exactly like something I'd do."

"I'd try to keep the route short," Anton added. "And I'd want to get off the highway as quickly as possible."

"Long Island, maybe?"

"Yeah," Anton agreed. "That would be a logical destination. I'd head for the Hampton's."

"You're talking money-country now. You'd need to blend in."

"With Lacey on my arm that wouldn't be hard."

"True. Car?"

"Something high-end. Lexus. Audi maybe."

"You think that sounds like the Scroll Killer's style?"

"Yeah, I do," Anton said. "The guy's smart and organized. Not only did he know exactly where to find Lacey, he's been able to avoid capture by the cops for months, maybe even years. That takes resources. I'm guessing he's independently wealthy. Which also means he's got time on his hands and the freedom to come and go whenever and wherever he pleases."

"That gives him quite a few travel options. Even a private jet. But a boat would make more sense. What better place to disappear than at sea? Lacey would have no chance of escaping from a boat."

"If I know Lacey like I think I do," Anton said, "she'd throw herself overboard and drown before she'd let him keep her as his captive."

"You thinking what I'm thinking?"

Anton nodded. "I know where I'd go."

"Montauk," they said, in unison.

Degario entered the Interstate ramp and stepped on the accelerator. In seconds, the men were cruising along the highway. He checked his rearview mirror. "Check it out," he said. "Behind us. Six car lengths back."

Anton turned in his seat, looked over his shoulder.

Even from a distance they could hear the thunderous roar of the Harley Davidson motorcycles. The six bikers rode side by side in groups of two.

"You think they're with us?" Anton asked. "Think they're looking for Lacey?"

Degario recognized the vest the men wore. Hells Angels.

"Count on it," he said. He tapped his brake lights: three times short, three times long, three times short. Morse code for S-O-S.

The lead bikes flashed their high beams and closed the distance to the car.

"Calvary's arrived," Degario said. "Now let's go find Lacey."

## 39

JORDAN PRESENTED HER credentials to the coroner. "I'd like to see the driver's body," she said.

The doctor stood beside the black hearse which contained the body of the decedent, Manny Manchescu. He nodded to his assistant. The man released the lock, swung open the back door, pulled out the loading platform on which Manny's body lay and unzipped the body bag.

The images came to Jordan fast and furious. Manny accompanying the woman in the wheelchair to the back of the apartment building... opening the door... lifting the chair into the tight vestibule... the violent assault with the wheelchair... blind panic as he fell, unable to grab hold of the stairwell handrail... his body falling, arms flailing... striking first his head, rendering him unconscious... tumbling down, down, down... the crack of his cervical vertebrae as he met the edge of each unforgiving step until finally slamming hard into the wall at the bottom of the stairs... the out-of-body experience when he realized death had come to carry him away... the white light... the terrifying presence of the dark profile that stood in front of it. Manny wanted to continue his journey to the other side, but the darkness was not finished with him. He felt the plunge of the knife into his dying body, the thrust of the steel blade inside him, twisting and tearing at his organs, pulled out of him, then driven in again and again. Soon the darkness faded, and the white light returned. For a second, he saw his wife and child, then traveled on. Serenity and peace came next, yet part of his energy remained, anchored to the foot of the stairs in the unfamiliar apartment building, realizing he was dead but unable to fathom why he was incapable of moving on. The spirit of Manny Manchescu was caught between the animated world of the living and the other-world of the dead.

Jordan placed her hand on the corpse's body. "I'm sorry," she said.

"About what?" the coroner's assistant asked curiously.

Jordan realized she had spoken her condolences aloud to the dead man. "Nothing," she replied. "Such a tragedy, that's all."

"Happens every day," the coroner replied nonchalantly. His associate zipped up the black bag, returned the corpse to darkness.

"Not three stab wounds and a broken neck," Jordan replied. "That's overkill. What else can you tell me about cause of death?"

"His shins are battered," the doctor said. "Causation is unknown at this time. But at first glance I don't think it was caused by the fall or by contact with the stairs. The injuries are in the same location on both legs. Which suggest to me that an implement of some kind was used. A stick or a bat, perhaps."

"Or the foldout footrests of a wheelchair?" Jordan offered.

The coroner considered her suggestion. "As a matter of fact, yes. Judging by the location of the wounds and approximating for height, impact from the footrests of a wheelchair could have caused the injuries to the victim's legs. That is plausible." The coroner looked perplexed. "What would lead you to believe a wheelchair was used in the attack?"

"We have an eyewitness that puts the victim in the company of another man and a woman in a wheelchair entering the building together through the rear entrance," Jordan explained. "The same location where the body was found."

Agent Penner joined the psychic and the coroner. To Jordan he said, "Your partner wants to see you. Says it's important."

Jordan nodded. She turned to the coroner, shook his hand. "Thank you," she said.

"You're welcome, Agent Quest," the doctor replied. "Contact me if you have any further questions."

"I will."

Jordan walked with Penner. "Agent Hanover found something beside the rear tire of the taxicab," he said.

"What is it?"

"A wedding band. There's an inscription."

"What does it say?"

"TDUDP. O."

"I think I know what that means," Jordan said.

"Me too," Agent Penner replied. "Till Death Us Do Part. But the 'O'?"

"If I had to guess," Jordan said, "I'd say it stands for 'Otto.'"

"Otto… as in the Scroll Killer?"

"That's right."

"Jesus," Penner said. "He doesn't want to kill her, does he?"

"No," Jordan said. "I think he wants to marry her."

## 40

LYING IN THE back seat of the Range Rover, Lacey tried to lift herself up, to look out the car window as they hurtled along the Interstate. Otto told her their destination was Montauk. She wanted to get her bearings, see where she was right now. The seat belts which bound her upper torso and legs were unforgiving. Hard as she tried, she could not see out the window. Straining to lift her body only resulted in the plastic zip ties cutting deeper into her skin. She examined her wrists. Blood. The constant chafing had broken the skin. Dark smears stained the gray leather upholstery. Good, she thought. If she didn't come out of this ordeal alive, the authorities would find blood in the vehicle. DNA testing would confirm it was hers and provide the evidence they would need to charge the sonofabitch behind the steering wheel with her abduction and murder. *Murder?* The word sent a chill down her spine. Oh hell, no. She would never let the situation get that far. She was Lacey *Fucking* Chastain, dammit. *She* was in control of her life, not this sick psychopath. You have him, she told herself. Keep playing him until he sets you free. Use everything you've got. Because it's now or never.

"Otto, please pull over."

"Not yet."

"It's urgent."

"Nothing is urgent, Lacey. We have all the time in the world."

"I have to pee," she lied.

Otto looked in his mirror. The woman looked uncomfortable. This was no way to treat his future wife. "All right," he said. "I'll take the next exit."

"Thank you."

"You're welcome. And sweetheart..."

"Yes?" Lacey replied.

"If you try to run, I'll kill you."

OTTO EXITED the Interstate at Old Westbury and followed the road to the nearest gas station, Speedy's. There he found a parking space far from the entrance to the combination gas station, convenience store, restaurant and truck stop which offered him the privacy he needed to deal with Lacey without being seen by the patrons of the small but busy establishment. An eighteen-wheeler chugged past the Range Rover as Otto backed in. He made eye contact with the trucker, smiled, flashed him a thumbs up. The driver nodded, waved, and replied with two shorts bursts of his air horn. Satisfied he was not being observed, Otto turned to Lacey. He removed his knife from its leg sheath and showed it to her. "I'm going to open the back door, release the seat belts and cut you loose," he said. "If you scream, you die. If you try to put up a fight or resist me, you die. Have I made myself clear?"

Lacey nodded.

"Good, because you won't get a second chance. I love you, Lacey. But I won't hesitate to kill you if I have to."

"I understand."

"All right. Now sit still and don't move."

Otto exited the car and surveyed the lot. All quiet. He opened the back door, leaned over Lacey, unbuckled the seat restraints that held her in place and cut loose the plastic ties which bound her wrists.

Lacey let out a sigh of relief. She massaged her wrists and hands. "God, they're sore."

"I'm sorry," Otto said. "It was necessary."

Lacey smiled. "I understand. You didn't know how I would react. I'd probably have handled the situation the same way if I were you."

"I'm glad you're not mad."

"Mad? No. Tired and hungry? Yes. Now, may I please use the bathroom?"

"Of course."

Keeping the knife to her back, Otto helped Lacey up and out of the car, then folded the weapon and placed it in his pocket. He held her by the arm, then pulled her to him, looked into her eyes. "Just another loving couple on a road trip to Montauk. That's the story if anyone asks. Got it?"

Lacey nodded.

"Good."

"Can we eat while we're here?" Lacey asked. "I'm starving."

Otto's voice was cold. "You're asking a lot."

"Only for food. You wouldn't let the woman you love go hungry, would you?"

Otto looked down. Lacey sensed his shame at the accusation. "Of course not."

"We could have something fast. Would a burger and fries be okay?"

Otto nodded. "All right."

"You order. I'll use the washroom. Then we'll eat."

Otto corrected her. "You'll use the washroom while I *wait* for you. Then we'll order and eat."

Lacey smiled. "Whatever you say."

"Good," Otto replied. He took her by the arm, held her tightly by his side. "Now move."

## 41

THE BIKE GANG sped up the Interstate, closed the distance, boxed in Mike and Anton. The gang leader motioned for him to lower his window. Degario complied.

"Everything all right?" the biker asked.

"Yeah, we're good," Mike replied. "You with the Long Beach chapter?" he asked.

The biker glanced apprehensively at the two men in the car. "Who are you guys? Feds?"

"Not too damn likely," Mike said. "We're on the same team. We're working with your boss, Blade. Or should I say he's working with us. We're looking for Lacey Chastain."

"The missing chick from the Odyssey. So are we."

Anton leaned forward, addressed the biker. "Where are you guys headed?"

"Blade told us to check out the truck stops along the Interstate. Just left Bayside. Next stop is Old Westbury."

Mike nodded in Anton's direction. "This is Anton Moore. He reported her missing. We should sit down when we hit Old Westbury. There's a gas bar and restaurant there named

Speedy's. We'll buy your guys a round. Anton can describe the asshole who took her to your men. Give you a better chance of finding the sonofabitch."

"Works for me," the biker said. He raised his hand in the air and pointed ahead. The Hells Angels raced ahead of Mike and Anton.

Anton stared out the window as the bikers whizzed past. "This is like trying to find the proverbial needle in a haystack," he said. "Lacey could be a hundred miles from us, headed in the opposite direction."

"That's true," Degario replied. "She could be. She could also be north of us. Or south. But she could also be in the very next car we see traveling beside us. You need to keep your head in the game, man. You said this girl means everything to you, right?"

"And then some."

"Then buck the fuck up and concentrate on finding her."

Anton chuckled. "You have such a way with words, Degario. You really know how to make a guy feel better."

"Screw feeling better," Mike said. "I want Lacey back as much as you do. Quit your whining and keep looking."

Anton reflected. "You know, the first forty-eight hours in a missing persons case are the most critical. After that, the chances of a positive outcome drop off exponentially. It's been almost forty-eight hours, Mike. We're gonna hit that cliff soon. And when we do, I don't know what I'll do if I find her at the bottom of it."

"If it makes you feel any better my gut says we're on the right track," Mike replied. "Besides, we still have a lot of climbing to do before we hit that cliff. I'm up for it. But the bigger question is, are you?"

Anton nodded. "Yeah, I am. All the way to the top."

"That's more like it."

The bikers were well ahead of them now, far down the highway, headed for Old Westbury.

Anton asked, "Can this thing go any faster, old man? Maybe I should drive."

"Very funny," Degario replied.

He hit the gas.

## 42

"UNIFORMS CANVASSING THE area around Kessel's Bookbinding just got a name for our guy in the hospital cam pic," Penner announced as he walked towards Jordan and Chris and returned his cellphone to its case. "Otto Schreiber. His late mother owned the company. Local business owners had seen him coming and going from the establishment. Told them he was making a few changes to the place and that it would be reopening in a few months."

"I suppose he neglected to tell them his reno included constructing a full-blown dungeon in the basement," Chris said.

"Apparently," Penner agreed. "But get this. The guy drives two cars. One is a Bentley, the other a silver Range Rover with a personalized license plate: MRGRIMM."

"Mrs. Sheen told us she'd caught part of the plate: MRG. She was right. The lady's a lot sharper than we gave her credit for."

"That's him," Jordan said. "Otto Schreiber *is* the Scroll Killer. The vanity plate is a sobriquet, a nickname. It all fits now. Like I said before, there is a strong correlation between the murders and the old stories penned by the brothers Grimm. Schreiber has a fascination with those tales. Probably sees himself in them. Except he's playing out the stories in real life."

"I'll get the license plate over the air," Chris said. "We need to use every resource we can to find that car: DMV, local and Interstate traffic cams, air support, state troopers and local law enforcement, BOLO's, the works."

"And pray to God Lacey's still alive when we do," Penner replied. "Jordan, you said you saw the word Montauk?"

"Yes," Jordan said.

"Montauk is the easternmost point of Long Island. There's nothing but Atlantic Ocean after that. If that is where he is headed, he just bought himself a one-way ticket to the end of the line. He'll have trapped himself. His ass is ours."

"We need a chopper," Chris said. "Who knows how much of a head start he has on us already."

"Consider it done," Penner said. He took out his phone, walked away, placed a call.

Chris handed Jordan the wedding ring. "I found this by the back tire of the cab. Think you could get a vibe from it that would help us find this guy?"

"I'll try," Jordan said. She took the ring, held it in her hand and closed her eyes. Images of Otto and his victims came into view. Lacey, Melinda, and Victoria imprisoned in the dungeon... the horrific murder and dismemberment of Courtney Valentine... the disemboweling of Rosalita Sanchez... Bonnie Cole laying drugged and unconscious on the surgical table, sections of her skin excised from her body... Manny Manchescu being pushed down the stairs, breaking his neck, dying where he lay... and Lacey, laying in the back seat of the Range Rover, precariously safe for the time being in the company of the serial killer. The vision suddenly changed. A beautiful young woman held an infant in her arms, crying from happiness, emotionally overwrought at the thought of being blessed with such a perfect gift. Jordan sensed the child was Otto, the woman his mother. The ring had been her wedding ring, now his to place on the finger of his future bride. The woman looked down at the baby. Through tears of joy, she whispered the words, 'Make it real, Otto... Make it real.' Suddenly Jordan felt uneasy, sick to her stomach. She opened her hand. The gold ring oozed blood. Maggots squeezed out from between the letters of the inscription, fell and wriggled on her palm.

Jordan gasped and dropped the ring.

Chris picked up the band from the ground. "You okay, Jordan?"

Jordan looked at the ring in Chris' hand. Bright and shiny. No blood, no maggots.

"What did you see?"

Jordan interpreted the symbolism of the vision for her partner. "He says he loves her, but he won't hesitate to kill her if she pushes him too far. He won't be able to stop himself. He is what he is. A murderer."

Penner joined them. "We need to leave. There is a park two blocks away. A chopper's en route to pick us up. It'll meet us there. We'll follow any leads from the air. You two ready?"

"We're good," Chris said.

Jordan thought of the young mother in her vision. Had she ever suspected that one day her infant son would grow up to be one of the most prolific serial killers the country had ever seen? How many more victims were out there, unaccounted for? For reasons she could not explain Jordan removed her service weapon from its holster, ejected the clip, checked it. Full. She slammed the clip back into the Glock. Something told her that before the day was out, she'd be putting the weapon to use.

"What was that for?" Chris asked as Jordan holstered her weapon.

"Peace of mind," she replied.

## 43

SPEEDY'S GAS STOP was a full-service operation. Otto and Lacey walked casually past the rows of eighteen-wheelers and exchanged pleasantries with several truckers. Otto held open the door for an elderly couple as they left the facility. When Lacey tried to step ahead of him, he grabbed her by her sore, damaged wrist, squeezed hard and pulled her back. Lacey winced and fought hard to not cry out at the unbearable pain. "Don't even think about it," Otto whispered.

"Thank you," the old woman said.

"You're most welcome, ma'am," Otto replied.

Through the entrance doors, a convenience store on the left offered an assortment of books, magazines, stuffed toys, chocolate bars, potato chips and soft drinks. Otto spotted the sign for the washrooms straight ahead and down the hall, WOMEN on the left, ACCESSIBLE in the middle, MEN on the right. The gas bar restaurant, Marnie's Fast Fuel, was located to the right of the front entrance.

"There," Otto said. He pointed to the washroom entrance at the end of the hallway. "I'll wait for you outside the door. If I hear you talking to anyone I'll come in, kill them first, then I'll kill you. Understand?"

"Yes," Lacey replied. She tried hard to control the anger in her voice. She wanted to put into practice what she had learned in her taekwondo classes; to pull her arm free from his iron grip, punch him as hard as she could in his throat, drive her knee repeatedly into his groin, then scream for help. Here, surrounded by many tough, burly truckers, one or more would be sure to rush to her defense. But Otto was armed with the knife, and no doubt knew how to use it. She couldn't allow innocent bystanders to die at his hand just to save her. No, she could handle this situation all on her own and would. If not now, soon.

Two truckers playing a video game in the corridor looked her up and down as she walked past. One man spoke to the other, then chuckled quietly to his friend. She could tell by their body language they were talking about her. Maybe she should call out the creep on his leering, use the opportunity to create a diversion, get away. No, she thought. To be guilty of being an asshole wasn't prerequisite enough to be knifed to death.

At the washroom entrance, Otto issued a demand. "Hug me," he said.

Lacey knew what was coming. Nevertheless, she did what she was told. Otto's hands explored the back pockets of her jeans and beneath them as he pulled her close. She felt the pressure of his body against hers.

Lacey smiled. "Satisfied?" she asked.

"That you're not concealing anything?" Otto replied. "Yes. Because if you had been, I would have taken that as a sign of mistrust. And what good is a relationship without trust, Lacey?"

Lacey wanted to tell him he was the one with the trust

issues but conceded the urge to do so. Instead, she replied, "Trust is everything, Otto. Like I said, you *can* trust me. I won't run. I won't leave you."

Otto smiled, then glanced at the washroom entrance. "Two minutes, then I come in. You don't want me to come in, Lacey."

Lacey smiled, stroked his face. "Give me a minute and a half."

Lacey walked in to find the washroom empty. Dammit! She looked under the stalls hoping to find someone to help her, someone with whom she could share the story of her abduction and tell the authorities. She investigated the room, tried to find a way out, found none. The ceiling vent in the middle of the room was large enough to accommodate her but impossible to reach without the aid of a stepladder. She needed to get help. But how? Of all the times for the washroom of a busy service center to be empty! Lacey entered the first stall and locked the door behind her. She needed something to write with, an implement with which she could scrawl a message into the back of the door. The pull tab on her zipper would have to do. Thirty seconds had already lapsed. Lacey took off her jeans, held the pants by the pull tab and furiously scratched a note into the gray paint.

LACEY CHASTAIN
KIDNAPPED
SILVER RANGE ROVER
CALL POLICE
NO JOKE

ONE-MINUTE LEFT...

Lacey quickly slipped back into her jeans. She overstuffed the toilet with wads of tissue and flushed.

Forty-five seconds...

She waited for the water to back up, flushed again. Water overflowed the toilet, spilling onto the bathroom floor

Thirty seconds...

Lacey opened the door, stepped out of the flooded stall, closed it quietly behind her, ran two stalls down and locked the door.

Fifteen seconds...

She heard voices, laughter. A group of women had entered the washroom.

Ten seconds...

She could rush out now, tell them her story, hope they would believe her.

*Five seconds...*

Ask for their help, tell them to call the authorities. Maybe one of them was armed. Maybe...

Suddenly one of the women called out. "Hey! What is your problem? Can't you read? The sign says WOMEN."

Lacey flushed the toilet and opened the door. Otto stood in the entranceway.

"I'm sorry, ladies," she lied. "He's my husband. I've been car sick. He's just checking up on me."

"That's right," Otto said. "Are you okay, honey?"

Lacey smiled. "I'm fine."

Otto addressed the women. "I'm sorry to have startled you, ladies. My wife has been in here a long time. Too long, in fact. I was getting concerned."

The tone in the room shifted. The angry woman relaxed. "I apologize," she said to Otto. "It's good of you to be concerned for your wife's well-being. I wish my husband was that attentive." To Lacey she said, "You're an incredibly lucky woman to have a guy like that. I'll bet he's one in a million."

Lacey washed and dried her hands and smiled. "You have no idea," she replied.

## 44

DEGARIO AND ANTON exited the Interstate at Old Westbury and pulled into the parking lot at Speedy's. The six Hells Angels assigned to search for Lacey stood beside their Harley's, waiting for the men to arrive, watching the people and vehicles as they came and went, on alert.

Degario recognized their leader, shook his hand. "Mike Degario," he said. "This is Anton Moore from the Odyssey."

"Sam Chapman," the biker answered, shaking Anton's hand. "The boys were pretty upset when they heard someone took your girl," he said. "Any leads?"

Degario shook his head. "We're doing all we can right now."

"We really appreciate your help," Anton said. "Can we buy you that round?"

Chapman smiled. "I'll never say no to a cold beer. Lead the way."

The men walked across the parking lot. The sunny day had clouded over. Grey skies threatened rain.

"What happened, exactly?" Chapman asked. "Why would someone want to take Lacey?"

Anton answered. "Truth is, we really don't know. First, we thought it was a bad date gone wrong. Now it looks like she was targeted by the Scroll Killer."

Chapman stopped and faced him. "The guy the cops are after? The serial killer?"

"The same."

"What makes you think you can find her if they can't?"

"Because when it comes to Lacey, I don't give a shit about the law. They have to play by the rules. I don't. Lacey's special to me and I want her back. And anyone who tries to hurt her is as good as dead."

Chapman nodded. "Good enough for me, brother," he said. "We've got your back."

"Thanks," Anton said. "Come on. Drinks are on me."

OTTO AND LACEY waited to be seated in Marnie's Fast Fuel, the restaurant section of the gas bar. Otto kept his arm around her, held her close. "Remember what I said, my love," he whispered in her ear. "Make a sound or try to run, I'll grab you and gut you like a fish... right here, right now. Clear?"

Lacey smiled as a young couple approached the cash register to pay their bill. "I understand," she said.

"Good," Otto said. "Have anything you want but eat it fast. We still have a couple of hours ahead of us."

The waitress approached. "Good day, honey," she said to Lacey. "For two?"

"Yes, please," Lacey replied.

"Come with me, darlin'. I'll set you up in a nice booth by the window."

Lacey and Otto followed the woman to the table and took their seats.

The waitress placed the menus on the table, took out her pencil and order pad. "Drinks to start?" she asked.

Lacey looked up, tried to make eye contact. The woman was staring intently at her pad, pencil poised, waiting.

"I'll have a…"

"…Two waters will be fine," Otto interrupted. "What's the fastest meal you've got?"

The waitress looked surprised.

Otto looked at the waitress's name badge. *Mabel.* "I'm sorry, Mabel," he said. "We're in a hurry."

Mabel smiled. "Then don't let us hold you up, sweetie. I'd recommend the grilled cheese and fries."

"Make it two."

Mabel scribbled the order on her pad. She laughed. "I wish all my customers were as easy to please as you two. Be back in a jiffy."

Damn it, Lacey thought. She wanted to get the woman's attention, communicate through eye contact that she was in trouble and in need of help. But Mabel was too wrapped up in doing a good job to notice.

The knives and forks on the table were neatly wrapped in serviettes. Lacey unraveled the napkin, removed the cutlery. Otto leaned forward, took the cutlery from her hand, placed it beside him on the bench seat. "You don't need a knife and fork for grill cheese and fries. Besides, you might be tempted to use them as weapons. You wouldn't have been thinking that, would you Lacey?"

Lacey wanted to answer him truthfully, tell him that was exactly what she was thinking of doing… of grabbing the utensils in both hands as tightly as she could then throwing herself across the table at him, driving the knife deep into his carotid artery, the fork into his throat, then run while he bled out and choked to death on his own blood.

Perhaps he was more of a match for her than she thought. He was cunning, alert, well-practiced, on top of his game. She would have to be patient, let the situation play itself out. When the time was right, she would strike back with every ounce of strength she had within her. But not now.

"Of course not," she replied. "Actually, I'm rather looking forward to the trip. I've never been to Montauk. Do you have a home there?"

"A yacht."

Lacey feigned excitement. "Really? I love being on the water! Where are we headed?"

"I'll make that decision when we're at sea."

"Can we go to the islands? The Bahamas maybe? I've always wanted to visit the Bahamas."

"We'll see."

"I can't wait."

"You're a bad liar, Lacey."

Lacey stared at Otto. Tears welled in her eyes.

"What's wrong?" Otto asked.

"You're not giving me a chance."

"A chance to what?"

Lacey dabbed her tears away on the paper napkin. "Love you," she said.

Otto took her hand in his. "We can't stay here, Lacey. It's too dangerous for me."

"I know."

"I want you to love me for all the right reasons. Not for the man I am but for the man you'll make me."

"I can't help you if you won't let me in."

"It's hard."

"I know."

"You'll just leave me too."

"No, I won't, Otto. You have to learn to trust me."

"I don't want to have to hurt you."

"Then don't."

Lacey looked up. A group of men walked across the parking lot. She stared closely, thought she recognized them. She did. Anton! Mike!

Otto glanced up, saw the look on her face, looked out the window. The sonofabitch from Lacey's apartment, the asshole who had shot him, was here. How could he have possibly known where to find him?

Otto was angry. "You did this," he said.

Lacey wanted to scream, throw something at the window, get their attention.

Otto grabbed her by her damaged wrist, pulled her up from the table. "Rear exit, past the washrooms," he said. "Move!"

Together they left Marnie's and headed for the back of the building.

"Bitch!" Otto said. "I knew you couldn't be trusted!"

## 45

NEW YORK STATE trooper Grant Malone heard the BOLO announcement on the police radio as he exited the Interstate ramp at Old Westbury. "All units. Be on the lookout for a silver Range Rover, New York license Montreal-Romeo-Golf-Romeo-India-Montreal-Montreal... M-R-G-R-I-M-M. Suspect is wanted for questioning by the Federal Bureau of Investigation and should be considered armed and dangerous. Suspect may be in the company of a Caucasian female, early twenties. Do not attempt to apprehend. Request immediate backup to your location."

As far as he was concerned, Marnie's Fast Fuel served the best homemade apple pie in all of New York State. Besides, he had a bit of a thing for the waitress, Mabel. She always made him feel at home whenever he dropped by. One of these days, when he finally worked up the courage, he would ask her out.

As was his habit, Malone always circled the parking lot to check out the vehicles before parking and taking his break. Prostitutes had been frequenting the rest stop lately, offering their services to long-haul truckers who parked their rigs at Speedy's overnight. The management of the facility had asked the police to step up their patrols in an effort to curtail the problem. Speedy's was a family-friendly, full-service gas station and restaurant chain. The ladies of the night were not welcome. Malone was under orders to either arrest them or move them along.

As he drove past two eighteen-wheelers, he spotted the Range Rover parked between them.

Malone braked, backed up the cruiser, and noted the license plate: MRGRIMM.

He spoke into his microphone: "4112 to dispatch."

The operator responded. "Go ahead, 4112."

"10-14. Can I get a read back on that Range Rover BOLO?"

"10-4. Silver, New York plates, license M-R-G-R-I-M-M."

"Copy that. Be advised I have a location on the vehicle. Requesting backup at—"

Otto thrust his knife through the open window of the squad car and plunged it deep into the officer's neck. Lacey screamed.

Otto double-clicked the Range Rover's remote, unlocked the doors. He hurried Lacey to the vehicle, threw open the driver's door, pushed her inside. "Crawl over!" he demanded. "Get in your seat! Do it now!"

Lacey stumbled over the center console and into her seat. "You killed him!" she screamed. "You killed that policeman."

"It was him or us."

"You bastard!"

Otto held the blade to her throat, wet with the fallen officer's blood. She felt it run down her neck, warm and thick. "Shut up! Shut up! Shut up!" he cried. Lacey could see he was devolving before her eyes. "This is all your fault! You could have stayed in the store with me, been happy. But no, that wasn't good enough for you. *I* wasn't good enough for you! You did that! Your fault, your fault, YOUR FAULT!"

Otto was losing his grip, unraveling. He pulled the knife away from Lacey's throat and slashed the leather dashboard with the blade, then pressed the tip of the weapon against her stomach. "Fuck that cop," he said. His breathing was heavy, his voice cold. "You'll listen to every word I say. Do you understand me? You know what that cop was? *Practice.* No one is going to take away what's mine. I have to make it right. Do you understand? I have to make it right!"

"What are you talking about?" Lacey asked. "Make *what* right?"

Otto returned the knife to its sheath. "Never mind."

In his cruiser, Trooper Malone lay slumped forward in his seat.

Otto eased the Range Rover past the police car and drove slowly across the parking lot. No one had followed them out of the rear exit of the service station or witnessed the attack.

With Speedy's Gar Bar behind them, Otto reached the ramp to the Interstate. "They'll be looking for us," he said. "We'll need to hurry."

"Give yourself up, Otto," Lacey urged. "This won't end well for you."

"You mean us."

"What?"

"It won't end well for *us*. Because whatever happens now happens to both of us. If I die, you die. Together forever, Lacey. Just like I promised. Together forever."

. . .

BACK IN THE parking lot at Speedy's, the police dispatcher asked Trooper Malone for his status. No response. The speaker in the officers patrol car announced, "Attention all units. Possible 10-13, officer requires assistance. Last known location Interstate 495 exit at Old Westbury. All available units respond, code three."

ROCKETING along the highway towards Montauk, the gravity of the situation struck Lacey. Right now, there was only one thing she could do to save herself from the madman seated beside her: cooperate.

Otto was determined not to let the murder of the police officer at the gas station dampen his mood. He turned on the radio, tuned in a classic rock station. Def Leppard sang, 'Pour Some Sugar On Me.'

He strummed the steering wheel with his fingers. The music made him feel better.

He turned to Lacey. "You know I only want to make you happy," he said. "That's all I've ever wanted."

Staring out the passenger window, Lacey turned and forced a smile. "I know, Otto," she said. "I know."

"I'm sorry."

"For what?"

"Killing the cop."

"I know you are."

"Do you forgive me?"

It was all she could do not to scream. Instead, she found the words. "Of course I forgive you," she said. "How could I not?"

# 46

*S*HOOP... SHOOP... SHOOP...

The agents watched and waited as the FBI Bell Ranger helicopter Penner had requested touched down. They ran to the bird, climbed aboard, buckled in, and put on their communications headsets.

Penner instructed the pilot. "Follow Interstate 495 east to Montauk."

"Copy that," the pilot said. "You looking for a specific target?"

"Silver Range Rover."

The pilot paused. "The BOLO? License plate 'MRGRIMM?'"

"Yeah," Penner replied. "Why?"

"State Police are responding to a call against that plate. A LifeFlight air ambulance has been called to the scene. Gas bar and restaurant in Old Westbury. State trooper was stabbed as he was calling it in."

"What's his condition?" Jordan asked.

"Chatter says he's bad, possibly critical."

"Schreiber," Chris said.

"Take us there," Jordan asked. "I want to see the scene."

"You got it," the pilot said. "Hang on."

The chopper lifted off the ground, circled the field, then swung right, headed east, picked up speed.

Within minutes they would be in Old Westbury.

## 47

ANTON AND DEGARIO entered Marnie's Fast Fuel restaurant together with Sam Chapman and his fellow Hells Angels members.

Mabel the waitress greeted them. "Help you boys?" she asked.

"Table for eight, please," Anton said.

"You betcha. Follow me."

Mabel seated the men by the window facing the highway. "What can I get you?" she asked.

"Eight beers to start," Anton replied.

"I've got Sam Adams on tap if you like. Seems to be a favorite here."

"That will be great."

Mabel smiled as she handed out the menus. "Coming right up."

Sam Chapman spoke to Anton. "What's the deal with this Chastain chick, anyway? Why did this guy target her?"

"No idea," Anton replied. "My guess is he visited the Odyssey, watched her perform, liked what he saw and decided he would abduct her. The rest I can't explain. All I know is that the guy's a psychopath. Lacey's in a lot of danger. We need to find her before he hurts her, or worse."

"We'll put him in the ground for this," Chapman said. "Nobody messes with Russ's girls and gets away clean."

"He's wounded," Anton said. "I'm pretty sure I clipped him."

"You shot him?" Chapman asked.

Anton nodded. "We had a run in at Lacey's apartment. I chased him, but he got away."

"What was he doing in her apartment?"

"No idea. He took me by surprise, tried to take me out, almost succeeded. When I find him he'll wish he had."

Mabel returned with a tray of beers. "Here you go, boys," she said. "This should take the edge off."

Sam Chapman opened his phone. He studied Lacey's picture, committed her face to memory.

Mabel looked at the image on the phone. Sam caught her staring at the picture. The waitress's affable disposition suddenly changed. She looked concerned.

"Something wrong, ma'am?" Sam asked.

"N-no," Mabel said.

Sam could tell she was lying. "Have you seen this girl?" he asked.

Mabel shook her head. "Please, I don't want any trouble," she said. "I don't want to get involved."

Anton took the phone from Sam and showed it to the waitress. "Please ma'am," he said. "If you've seen her you need to tell us. It's very important."

"What did she do?" Mabel asked.

"Absolutely nothing," Degario interjected. "We're trying to find her, to help her. We believe her life may be in danger."

Mabel looked nervous. "I don't know," she said.

"Please," Anton said. "She's very important to me. We believe she's been kidnapped."

"*Kidnapped?*" Mabel exclaimed. "Oh, my goodness."

"Which is why we need to know if you've seen her," Degario said. "Can you help us?"

Mabel looked across at the empty table. "She was here," she said. "She was with a man. I brought their lunch to the table, but they'd left the restaurant."

"This man," Anton said. "Can you describe him?"

"White," Mabel said. "Early thirties, good looking. He was wearing jeans and a blue sweatshirt. It had a stain on the shoulder. Looked like dried blood, like maybe he'd hurt himself."

"Did you see them leave?" Degario asked.

Mabel shook her head. "I was in the kitchen picking up their order. As you can see, we're very busy."

"How long ago was this?" Anton asked.

"Five minutes… ten at the most."

Degario stood to leave. "That doesn't put them very far ahead of us," he said. "If they've come here, we know they're traveling east. If we leave now, there's a chance we can catch up to them."

Anton threw enough money on the table to cover the drinks. He handed Mabel a one-hundred-dollar bill. "Thank you, ma'am."

The men stood to leave.

"One more thing," Mabel said. "The way he acted. It was odd."

"What do you mean?" Anton asked.

"He ordered for her. Wouldn't let the poor dear speak. I thought perhaps they had had an argument or something. You know how couples can be sometimes. Waiting on tables you see it all. People don't think we pick up on these things, but we do."

"You've been very helpful, Mabel," Degario said. "Thank you."

"I hope she'll be all right," Mabel said as the men started to leave.

"So do we," Anton replied.

Outside the restaurant, a small crowd had gathered around a police car parked at the far end of the lot. The officer had been removed from his vehicle. He lay on the ground. A man was leaning over him, performing CPR.

In the distance, emergency sirens wailed, grew louder. Police cars raced to a stop, blocked the entrance to Speedy's Gas Bar.

Above them, approaching fast, the steady thrum of an inbound helicopter grew louder.

The men watched as the Interstate traffic braked to a halt behind an armada of police cars.

A LifeFlight air ambulance helicopter cleared the top of the restaurant, started its decent and set down on the highway entrance ramp to Speedy's. The paramedics disembarked from the chopper, off-loaded a gurney, and ran to the location of the fallen officer.

"They're shutting down the Interstate," Anton said. "We need to leave, now."

## 48

LACEY WAS QUIET as they left Old Westbury and traveled east on Interstate 495, her thoughts returning to the panicked look on the face of the state trooper when he turned his head, too late, to acknowledge his attacker. Otto had acted swiftly, plunged the knife deep and fast into the officer's neck before he had the chance to notify his dispatcher of the danger he was in. He had tried to speak, couldn't, dropped his radio microphone, and raised his hands to his neck in a futile effort to stop the bleeding. All she could do was watch in fear. She wanted to run to the officer, throw open the door, apply direct pressure to the wound, grab his radio, call for help. But the scream that had escaped her was involuntary, born of terror from having witnessed such a heinous and despicable act.

"You'll like living on the yacht."

Lacey's mind was a million miles away from the conversation. "Huh?" she answered.

"The sea," Otto said. "There's a peace and serenity about it you can't quite put into words. You'll like living on the water. No one around for miles. The occasional visit from a seagull. It's the perfect place to discover yourself, to learn who you truly are."

Lacey forced a smile. "It sounds wonderful," she lied.

"Have you been before?"

"Where?"

"To sea."

"No," Lacey said.

"Then I'll make it special for you," Otto said. There was excitement in his voice. "Do you still want to go to the Bahamas?"

"Where?"

"An hour ago. Back at the restaurant. You asked me if we could go there. That you *wanted* to go there. You weren't lying about that, were you?"

Lacey took his hand. She replied as convincingly as she could. "Of course not. The Bahamas, Bermuda, Turks & Caicos… wherever the weather's warm. I'm tired of the cold New York winters. It's time for a change. The more I think about it the more I realize how right the timing was for you to come into my life. I don't just want this. I *need* this. All the better that I get to spend it with you."

Otto smiled. Her response sounded genuine. "I'm glad you feel that way."

Lacey patted his hand and smiled. "Me too," she said. She looked out the window. "How long before we get to Montauk?"

"An hour and a bit," Otto said. They had exited the Interstate at Brentwood and were now heading south to Brightwaters. "Traffic's light. We'll be there before you know it."

Lacey struggled to find something to talk about, to keep her mind off her kidnapping and the tumultuous events of the day. "Tell me about your boat," she said.

"It's not a boat," Otto said. "It's a yacht."

"There's a difference?"

"Huge."

Who the fuck cares, Lacey thought. Instead, she asked, "Like what?"

"Amenities, accommodations, communications, nautical range," Otto said. "Her name is *Ava's Dream*. She belonged to my late mother. One-hundred-and-forty-seven feet of perfection. Twin diesel engines, almost fifteen-thousand-gallon fuel capacity. She'll take us anywhere we want to go."

Anywhere except home, Lacey thought. "Do you miss her?" she asked.

"Who?"

"Your mother."

Otto paused. "Every day."

"Do you think she would have liked me?"

"She would have loved you."

"Why?"

"Because you're good for me. You make me want to be a better man."

"You're already a good man, Otto," Lacey lied. "Deep down. Your intentions are good."

"I've killed people."

"I know."

"Many people."

Lacey was growing weary of keeping up the facade. Otto was not a good man, not by a long shot. She was only telling him what she felt he needed to hear to prolong her own life even if just for the moment. Back at Speedy's, he had likely killed the police officer. In the dungeon in Kessell's he had nearly taken the life of Bonnie Cole and was prepared to do the same to Melinda and Victoria. Now Bonnie lay in hospital, either recovering from her injuries or fighting for her life, and thankfully Melinda and Victoria were safe. She would have to get away from him before they reached Montauk. Once at sea there would be no escape. She would be trapped. His to do with as he pleased. A prisoner on the water.

"Can we open the windows, Otto? I need fresh air," she said.

"I'll turn up the air conditioning."

Lacey sensed his suspicion. "I'd really prefer to feel the breeze on my face. Please?"

"I suppose," he said. "But only for a little while."

Lacey pressed the button on her armrest console and lowered the window. She lay back in her seat, closed her eyes, breathed in the cool afternoon air, and placed her arm on the windowsill.

"What a perfect day," she said. She needed to engage Otto in conversation, allay any feelings of mistrust he might still have of her.

"How long does it take to prepare the yacht to leave?" she asked. "I'm tired." She extended her hand out the window then rested it on the sill.

Otto glanced at her. "Ten minutes," he said. "I always keep her gassed up and ready to go."

Lacey rested her feet on the knife-slashed dashboard, cupped her palm, and allowed the force of the airstream racing past the car to lift and drop it playfully.

"What are you doing?" Otto asked.

Lacey smiled. "Having fun," she said. She lowered her hand, placed it against the dust-covered door. With her fingertip she drew a number: 9.

"Put your arm back in the car," Otto said.

"Why? What's the matter? I'm just enjoying myself." Another number: 1.

"Don't make me tell you again."

A third: 1.

"All right, all right," she said. "No need to get so uptight about it. I don't see the harm in—"

Otto struck her across the face with the back of his hand. The impact stunned her. "The next time I tell you to do something, do it."

The blow cut her lip. Lacey tasted blood. If she could have, she would have killed him then and there.

With a whirring sound the window retracted.

Lacey pulled her arm back inside the car.

From his console, Otto pushed the master all window lock button.

*Click.*

# 49

JORDAN, CHRIS, AND AGENT PENNER looked down from the FBI chopper at the organized chaos unfolding below them at Speedy's Gas Bar in Old Westbury. State and local police had shut down the highway and the entrance and exit to the facility. Curious motorists stood outside their vehicles, trying to catch a glimpse of the action as it unfolded beyond the yellow and black crime scene tape that encircled the restaurant and parking lot. Jordan watched the blades of the LifeFlight air ambulance begin to rotate, heard the whine of its engine as it prepared for takeoff. As paramedics and fellow officers rushed a horrifically injured Trooper Malone to the bird, its rotor speed increased as the chopper waited impatiently to receive its patient. Seconds later, with all parties now safely aboard, the aircraft lifted off and began its ascent. Clear of the scene, the machine picked up speed. Its destination: Stony Brook Southampton Hospital Trauma Centre.

The FBI pilot spoke: "Hold on. I'm taking her down."

The helicopter landed on the northeast corner of the parking lot outside the barricade of police cars and emergency vehicles which surrounded the gas station. Jordan slid open the side door and stepped out of the chopper, followed by Chris and Agent Penner. "Keep her warm," Penner yelled above the roar of the engine. The pilot nodded, gave a thumbs up.

As the agents reached the site of the attack, crime scene investigators were analyzing Trooper Malone's cruiser, photographing the scene, laying down evidence markers on the bloody ground where the two truckers, upon returning to their rigs, spotted the injured officer, pulled him out of his squad car, and administered CPR in an effort to save his life.

Jordan presented her credentials to the trooper standing beside the vehicle. "How's your man doing?" she asked.

State Trooper Sergeant Leslie Mallory introduced herself, shook her hand. "Not good," she replied. "He's lost a lot of blood. Paramedics said the wound appeared to be major, likely from a knife attack, but they couldn't be sure. Depth and path of the penetration is unknown. He was spitting up blood when they were working on him and air bubbles were forming around the wound. They suspect his airway had been compromised, that his trachea shifted because of the attack." Mallory looked away. "It should have been me, you know," she said. "Grant and I switched breaks. He said he wanted to catch Mabel when she went off shift."

"Mabel?"

"She's a waitress here. Grant likes her, wanted to ask her out."

"Does she know what's happened?"

"Just that an officer was hurt. We're trying to keep the details quiet for now. I plan to tell her in a few minutes. Grant would want her to know."

"Anyone see the attacker?"

Mallory shook her head. "He or she got away clean.

There are cameras in the lot. I have men going over them now. Strange though."

"What is?"

"One of the custodians demanded to speak to an officer. He seemed pretty shook up. We thought it had to do with Grant's attack, but it didn't. Someone wrote a note on the back door of one of the washroom stalls. Said she'd been kidnapped and to call the police."

Chris and Penner joined Jordan as she spoke to the trooper. "What did the note say?"

Mallory removed her notepad, read back the notation: "Lacey Chastain. Kidnapped. Silver Range Rover. Call police. No joke." She closed the book, shook her head. "We told him not to worry about it. Unfortunately, that kind of nonsense happens more times than you'd care to know about. Some people get their kicks in the weirdest ways."

Jordan was angry. "That's no joke, Sergeant," she said. "Lacey Chastain is why we're here. And I strongly suspect it was the Scroll Killer who attacked your officer."

"Jesus," Mallory said. "I didn't think..."

"That's right," Penner interjected, chastising her. "You didn't *think*. Look, I'm sorry as hell that one of your officers went down in the line of duty and I pray to God he'll be okay. But not taking that note seriously? What the hell were you thinking?"

"I'm sorry, agents," Mallory said. "I truly am. I won't ever let it happen again."

Jordan nodded. "All right. Take me to that stall. I want to see it for myself."

"Follow me," Mallory said.

. . .

JORDAN STEPPED into the washroom and ran her hand over the message scratched into the metal door. *Lacey entering the restaurant... the knife to her back... her unbridled fear at the thought of being caught by Schreiber while leaving the note... fighting for emotional control... don't panic... Montauk... Montauk...*

The connection, a flash of images presented to her instantly, was lost.

"It's legitimate," Jordan told Chris, Penner and Sergeant Mallory. "It's not a prank. Lacey left this message. She and Schreiber were here."

"The BOLO," Chris said.

Penner nodded. "That's why Trooper Malone was attacked," he agreed. "He heard the 'be on the lookout' call, recognized the plates. Schreiber must have caught him off guard. I'm surprised he didn't kill him."

"He sure as hell tried," Jordan replied.

Knock-knock.

A police officer stood at the entrance door to the restroom. "Excuse me," he said. "Are you the agents with the FBI?"

"We are," Jordan replied.

"There's a woman out here who wants to talk to you. A waitress. Name is Mabel. She says it's important."

"We'll be right there," Jordan said.

"We'll need someone from maintenance to remove this door," Penner instructed Sergeant Mallory. "It's evidence. I'll need your people to secure it and have it couriered to the FBI New York field office."

"You've got it," Mallory said. "The woman asking for you is the one Trooper Malone was coming to see, Mabel Barillo. I need to break the news to her about Grant. She'll be crushed."

"Very well," Jordan said. "We'll speak to her first. Perhaps you can arrange for her to go to the hospital, wait for him until he comes out of surgery."

"She'd appreciate that," Mallory replied.

Mabel Barillo was nervous. "I'm so sorry," she said. "I hope I'm not wasting your time."

"We're happy to speak to you, Ms. Barillo," Jordan said. "What did you want to tell us?"

"I was waiting on a table earlier before this whole situation happened outside. A group of men had come in for a drink. Bikers, plus a couple who weren't."

"Go on."

"One of them showed me a picture on his cell phone of a young woman."

"And?"

"He said they were looking for her. That she had been kidnapped, and they were trying to find her."

"What did this man look like?" Penner asked.

"Tall... muscular... handsome... African-American. One of the men mentioned him by name... Anton."

Penner turned to Jordan and Chris. "Anton Moore."

"He's going after Lacey," Chris said. "If he catches up to them before we do..."

"Schreiber will kill him," Jordan finished.

"Thank you, ma'am," Penner said. "You've been very helpful."

The agents turned to leave.

Jordan watched Sergeant Mallory take Mabel by the arm and lead her to a nearby table. "Ms. Barillo," she heard her say. "I think you better sit down. I'm afraid I have some very bad news to tell you."

# 50

MIKE DEGARIO DROVE behind the bikers as they traveled east along the Interstate. Anton sat in quiet contemplation, staring out the window. Finally, he spoke. "You think we're wasting our time?"

"What is that supposed to mean?" Mike answered.

"This whole pursuit is a roll of the dice," Anton said. "We don't know what kind of car Lacey is in, whether they're still on the highway, nothing."

"You're right," Mike said. "But here's what we *do* know. We just missed her. The waitress confirmed it. Yeah, they've got a head start on us, but not by much. And we've got dozens of guys from three clubs out looking for her covering everywhere from here to Jersey, all of them with orders to find Lacey. We might be up against the wall, but it's temporary. We'll find her."

"You think the police activity back at the restaurant had something to do with this?"

Degario shrugged. "Dunno. It would be one hell of a

coincidence if it hadn't. The action was centered on the cop on the ground."

"You think Scroll attacked him?"

"If he did, that would play in our favor," Mike said.

"How do you figure?"

"If Scroll took him out the cops are going to pull out all the stops to find him. They'll throw up a perimeter, set up roadblocks, the works. He'd have to be one lucky sonofabitch to slip past them."

"Assuming they even know who they're looking for," Anton said. "He's been able to avoid capture for years. I don't think a few roadblocks will stop him."

Ahead, Sam Chapman waved his hand, pointed to the side of the road.

"Looks like Sam wants to talk," Degario said. He followed the bikers off the Interstate, pulled in behind them.

Chapman spoke with his men, then walked back to the car. Degario lowered his window.

"We may have something," he said.

"What's that?"

"I got a call. Two of our guys spotted a silver Range Rover about fifty miles from here. A man and a woman are in the vehicle."

"Did they recognize Lacey?" Anton asked.

Chapman shook his head. "They can't confirm if it's her, but they believe she's in trouble."

"How's that?"

"Someone wrote '9-1-1' in the dust on the door panel. They were going to approach the car and challenge the driver but decided it would be better if they stayed back and kept an eye on the car for the time being."

"Where are they now?" Degario asked.

"Got off the Interstate five minutes ago at Brentwood.

They're passing through Brightwaters. Looks like they're headed for Highway 27."

"Tell them to stay with them," Anton said. "Wouldn't you want to get as far off the highway as you could if you thought the cops were looking for you?"

"In a heartbeat," Chapman said.

"Makes sense," Degario said. "That's the Sunrise Highway. There will be minimal traffic on that route. He would want to go someplace with little police presence. Montauk could offer that. And it's at the end of 27."

"He's hiding in plain sight," Degario said.

"Exactly," Anton agreed.

"Want my guys to stop the car and check on the girl?" Chapman said.

Anton shook his head. "It's too dangerous. Tell them to hang back and keep the car in sight. Let them know we're on our way. We'll follow you."

"You got it."

"Thanks, Sam," Degario said.

Chapman spoke to Anton. "Told you we'd find her," he said.

Anton nodded. "Inform your men we're taking him down the first chance we get. As soon as Lacey's safe, he's mine."

"Everyone wants a piece of this guy," Chapman replied.

"They're welcome to play," Anton said. "But not before I've had my turn."

## 51

OTTO AND LACEY traveled east on Sunset Hwy 27 from Brightwaters. In Eastport, traffic was reduced to a single lane. Many car lengths ahead, police lights flashed.

Speedy's, Otto thought. The dead cop.

The manhunt was on.

Otto removed his knife from its sheath, opened the blade and rammed its tip into the driver's door armrest, keeping the weapon within arm's reach should the police stop him and instruct him to lower his window. At close range, the knife would easily penetrate the officer's bullet-proof vest. The cop wouldn't stand a chance. The strike, center-vest and directed upward toward the heart, would kill him instantly.

Cars whizzed past in the opposite direction. Otto considered doing a U-turn and finding an alternate route that would take them into Montauk. No, he thought. Play it out. If the police stopped the Range Rover, he would take the fight to them and put his extensive killing experience to work. Overpower the closest cop. Cut his throat. Take his weapon. Open fire. Press the attack. Drop them all. Disable their vehicles. Confiscate their bodycams. Make clean his getaway. By the time backup arrived he and Lacey would be long gone. No one would be left alive to inform their fellow officers of the direction in which they had fled.

Lacey sat forward in her seat and stared at the sea of emergency lights up ahead.

Otto issued a warning. "You want to see another cop die today?"

Lacey looked at Otto. "Don't," she replied.

"Then sit back and shut up. I'll handle this. Remember what I said earlier. You make a sound, you die. You don't want a cop's death on your conscience, do you?"

"No."

"Good."

Twenty cars ahead, an officer spoke briefly to a driver, then waved him through.

"How long until we get to the yacht?" Lacey asked.

Sixteen cars.

"An hour and a bit," Otto said. He wrapped his hand around the knife handle. "Why?"

Fourteen cars.

Distract him, she thought. "Can we stop before we get there?"

"Why?"

Twelve cars.

"I'll need to shop, pick up a few things."

"Everything you'll need is on the yacht. I've seen to it."

Nine cars.

"How could you possibly know—"

"Your clothing sizes? I've been watching you for a very long time, Lacey. Everything else I picked up from your apartment."

*You've been in my fucking apartment?* Lacey thought.

Seven cars.

"There are… other things," Lacey continued.

"Such as?"

"You know."

Five cars.

"Women-specific products."

Four cars.

"On the yacht. I've thought of it all."

The cop waved two vehicles through, spoke to the driver of the third, sent him on his way. He waved at Otto, instructing him to pull ahead, motioning for him to lower his window.

Otto pulled the knife out of the armrest, held it tight, readied the angle for a quick attack.

"Please," Lacey said. "Don't."

Otto lowered the window as the officer approached the car.

Ahead of the police cars, two vehicles lay twisted and entangled in the middle of the road. The traffic accident had been catastrophic, likely fatal for one or both parties.

"Remember," Otto whispered. "Utter a sound and he dies."

The cop leaned over and spoke. "Good day, sir."

"Afternoon, Officer," Otto said.

"Be careful for the next quarter mile," the cop said. "Slow it down. Keep a close eye on the road. The debris field is extensive. You don't want to blow out a tire."

No manhunt, no blockade. Just a traffic accident. Otto let go of the knife, raised his hand, waved.

"Much appreciated, Officer," he said. "Thanks for the warning."

"All right," the cop said. "Drive safely."

The policeman stepped away from the car, directed his attention to the vehicle behind Otto, motioned for the driver to pull ahead.

Lacey looked at the accident scene. Tarpaulins lay over the driver's doors of both cars. Twin fatalities, no doubt.

Otto eased the Range Rover around the pieces of broken plastic, metal, and glass scattered across the road. "Just think, Lacey," he said. "Judging by where we were in the cue of cars ahead of us, that could well have been us."

Lacey wanted to say she wished it had, that such a terrible death would be welcome right now, a blessing compared to the thought of spending another second in the company of the man seated beside her. Instead, she said, "Maybe you have your mother to thank."

"What do you mean?" Otto replied.

"Perhaps she's looking out for you, for us. Maybe we were meant to stop at the gas station, to be delayed long enough that we would avoid being in an accident."

Otto nodded. "You're right," he said. "Her spirit is with us, watching over us. Yes, that must be it. It was divine intervention."

"What other reason could there be?" Lacey said.

"That was very insightful," Otto said.

"Thank you."

"It means a lot to me that you would think of that."

"Like your mother, Otto, I have only your best interests at heart."

"I wish you had known her."

"Me too," Lacey lied. "She'd have been proud of you for not killing that policeman."

Otto nodded in agreement. "Yes, she would have."

"Can we stop soon?"

"We'll be in Montauk shortly."

"Just for a minute?"

"Sit back, Lacey."

"But..."

"The next time we stop we'll be at the yacht."

"But I need..."

"Nothing," Otto said. "You need absolutely *nothing*." He raised his hand. "Now be good. Don't make me discipline you again."

Lacey stared at him. *Discipline her?* She wanted to dive across the seat, grab the knife, yank it free of the armrest, plunge it repeatedly into his body before he had time to react, then throw open the passenger door, dive onto the roadway, roll, roll, roll free of the car and watch as it careened out of control, flipped over and over and over until it exploded and burst into flames, consuming Otto Schreiber in the process and taking him back to the Hell from which he had surely come.

Instead, she acquiesced, did as she was told.

Shaking with silent rage, Lacey sat back in her seat.

His death would have to wait.

## 52

AIRBORNE ONCE AGAIN, the FBI helicopter followed the Interstate in search of the silver Range Rover.

"You sure about Montauk?" Chris asked Jordan over the communications headset.

Jordan nodded. "Positive. That's where they're headed."

Penner had been patched into an outside line. He ended the conversation. "That was Pallister. NYPD found Schreiber's second car, the Bentley, abandoned in a convenience store parking lot. Forensics is going over it now. There are bloodstains in the trunk."

"Courtney Valentine?" Chris asked.

"And others, no doubt," Penner answered, "plus some weird shit. A black cape, masquerade mask, vocal synthesizer, rope, zip ties, garbage bags... the list goes on."

"Melinda and Victoria said he kept his appearance and voice disguised," Jordan said. "The rest sounds like the makings of an abduction kit."

Penner nodded, then added. "I called Bellevue. Bonnie Cole's husband made it to the hospital. He's with her now.

The docs say she's stable, out of the woods. It'll take a while for her wounds to heal but they expect she'll make a full recovery."

"Physically, anyway," Chris said. "It'll take years for her to get over the psychological trauma of her ordeal."

"Bonnie's one of the strongest women I've ever met," Jordan said. "She's a survivor. If anyone can get through this she can."

"NYPD also found Father Frank, or should I say his body," Penner continued. "He was shot twice, once in the chest, once in the head. Body was left in a Dumpster. A sanitation crew watched it fall into the back of their truck. Shook them up pretty good, poor bastards."

"Schreiber's tying up loose ends," Chris said.

Penner nodded. "Or someone associated with him."

From his pocket Chris removed the wedding band he had found beside the taxicab at the Conroy Apartments and examined it.

"Can I see that Chris?" Jordan asked.

"Sure," Chris replied. He passed the ring to his partner.

The psychic energy the band exuded was stronger now than during the previous connection and centered on Schreiber. He had kept it with him for as long as he'd been watching Lacey, waiting for the right time to present it to her. *Water... the campus at NYU... water everywhere, as far as the eye could see... sitting in the darkest corners of the Odyssey, watching her perform... Ava's Dream, motoring along the Atlantic coast... stalking her in the grocery store... the back seat of the Bentley... Lacey in the strappado... breaking into her apartment...*

Water... there was something significant about the water.

"Agent Penner," Jordan said, "you said earlier that if

Schreiber was headed to Montauk, he'd have trapped himself."

Penner nodded. "Unless he plans to disappear at sea there's nowhere left for him to go."

"That's it," Jordan said.

"What is?"

"Ava's Dream."

"What are you talking about?"

"There's a yacht... *Ava's Dream*. I saw it. That's where he's headed. We need to run a search on that vessel. Find out where it's moored in Montauk."

"On it," Penner said. He connected his phone to the choppers control panel cellular interface, placed a call to the Montauk Harbor Patrol.

Jordan spoke to Chris. "If you were Scroll and running from the police what route would you take?"

"I'd stick to the coastline and small towns," Chris replied.

"Then that's what we need to do." To the pilot Jordan said, "Other than Interstate 495, what's the most direct route into Montauk?"

"27," the pilot answered. "The Sunset Highway. It'll take you straight in."

"Take us there."

"Copy that," the pilot replied. The helicopter banked right, assumed a new southeasterly heading.

"Got it," Penner said. "There's a motor yacht by the name of Ava's Dream moored at Garney's Resort and Marina in Montauk."

"That's it," Jordan said. "We need to get to Garney's. He's using the yacht to escape."

"And he's taking Lacey with him," Chris finished.

## 53

SAM CHAPMAN'S PHONE rang.

"We've got the Range Rover in sight," Henny Black reported. "Eastbound on Sunrise Highway at East Hampton. There's an accident ahead. Radio says it's a bad one, twin-fatality. Cops have set up a safety checkpoint. They're letting us through one at a time. Hold on..." The Hells Angel straddled his Harley over the lane to get a closer look. "The Rover's clear now. He's on the move."

"We're on our way," Chapman said. "Stay with him."

Chapman gunned the engine. The motorcycle picked up speed, surged ahead. His fellow gang members followed close behind.

Degario sped up, closed the gap, stayed with them. They were now traveling well above highway speed.

"Something's up," Anton said.

"Yeah," Degario agreed. "Sam must have gotten a call. We must be getting close to Scroll and Lacey."

"I hope so," Anton said, "because there's nothing like rocketing down the highway on the ass of a band of Hells Angels to draw attention to yourself."

Ahead, a trail of red brake lights. The traffic had slowed to a crawl.

Chapman and his men slowed, stopped. Sam hopped off his bike, walked back, updated the men. "They just cleared the accident site," he said. "Our guys are on them."

"Good," Degario said.

"You think he knows he's being followed?" Anton asked. "If you spook him, he might hurt Lacey."

Sam shook his head. "I doubt it. He's watching out for cops, not us. And my guys are pros. They could roll right up beside him and not let on he's their target. Come to think of it, maybe that should be the plan."

"What?" Anton asked.

"Pull up beside him, cap him, get Lacey."

"It's a nice thought," Anton said, "but it's too risky. If they make their move and the play goes south Lacey is dead. No, we need to wait. After she's out of harm's way I don't give a shit what you do to him."

The traffic began to move.

"Stay on my six," Sam said. He walked back to his bike, revved the engine, put the machine in gear, drove off.

Degario drove ahead. Police waved them past the mangled wreckage which had now been placed onto a flatbed trailer parked on the side of the road.

The road now clear, Anton and Degario raced along the highway. The bikers accelerated, opened the gap.

Overhead, a helicopter raced past.

Degario looked up, identified the chopper by its markings. "FBI," he said.

"They're after the Range Rover," Anton said. "If Scroll makes the chopper, sees he's being followed..."

"... Lacey is as good as dead," Degario finished.

He hit the gas.

## 54

GARNEY'S MARINA WAS quiet. Otto pulled into the parking lot. He retrieved the knife, pointed it at Lacey. "Here's what will happen," he said. "You'll wait for me to open your door and let you out of the car, then you'll walk with me to the yacht. You don't look at anyone. You don't talk to anyone. Car to the yacht. Got it?"

Lacey nodded, said nothing.

Berthed at the end of the pier, the motor yacht Ava's Dream sat dead steady in the calm Atlantic water.

"There's a security gate ahead," Otto said. "When we reach it, you'll hold onto it with both hands while I enter the key code, then you'll walk to the end of the pier and get on the yacht. Challenge me in any way and you'll wear the knife." He pointed out to sea. "The Atlantic might be beautiful, but the waters along this coast are dangerous as hell. Can you swim?"

"Yes," Lacey said.

"Good," Otto said. "Not that it would matter. You'd be dead within a minute."

"Why?"

"Doesn't matter. Let's just say it wouldn't be pleasant. Now sit there and wait."

Otto stepped out, walked around the Range Rover, opened Lacey's door, grabbed her by the arm, pulled her out of the car, pointed to the middle of the pier. He saw what she had written on the dusty door: *911*. "Bitch," he said. "The gate. Move!"

Lacey stood beside the vehicle. Otto lowered the knife, exposed himself. One well-placed side kick, she thought. Aim for his solar plexus. Drive the blade of her foot deep into his chest. The crushing blow would incapacitate him instantly. She could make a run for it, try to escape.

Otto stepped out of the line of attack. The opportunity had been missed.

"Keep your back to me," he said as he closed the car door. "Feel that?"

Through her clothes, Lacey felt the tip of the knife against her back.

"Yes."

"You'd be surprised how little force is needed to break the skin," Otto said. "After the initial penetration, a quick twist at this angle and your spinal cord will be severed. You'll drop to the ground and never get up again, paralyzed from the neck down. You don't want that, do you Lacey?"

"No."

"I didn't think so. I wouldn't want that for you either. We have too much living to do, you and I."

"I'm looking forward to it, Otto," Lacey replied. "Please move the knife. It hurts."

In the distance came the roar of motorcycles. The sound grew louder, steel thunder. The bikers rolled up to the main entrance of the marina, stopped, their machines idling.

Otto watched them dismount, turn, and speak to one

another. They appeared to be searching for something or someone. Otto recognized the emblem on the back of their vests. What were four members of Hells Angels doing at Garney's?

No matter. In a moment he and Lacey would be free of the dock. Ava's Dream would set out to sea. The Bahamas awaited.

The biker walked ahead, looked at Otto, took out his phone.

The four men angled their bikes, blocking the exit to the yacht club, then turned off their engines, stepped off the machines, and started to walk in their direction.

Otto's every instinct told him these men were trouble, that somehow they were coming for him. Obeying his sixth sense, he pushed Lacey forward. "Start walking," he said.

Lacey walked ahead of Otto down the gangway to the security gate and placed her hands on the metal bars as she had been instructed. Otto entered the key code. With a *click* the door opened.

A voice called out from behind. "Lacey? Lacey Chastain?"

Lacey turned around. The bikers were advancing. One of the men held a gun at his side.

Otto pushed her through the open gate, stepped through, then closed and locked the steel door behind him. He grabbed Lacey, spun her around, placed the knife to her neck, issued a warning to the bikers. "Another step and she dies!"

Henny Black raised his hand. The men stopped. "Give it up, man," Henny yelled.

"Drop the gun," Otto said.

"Never gonna happen," Henny replied.

Otto called out. "Did you come here to save her or to watch her die?"

The biker raised his hands, showed Otto the gun.

"Toss it," Otto said.

"No!" Lacey cried.

Otto pressed the knife to her throat, cut her skin. Warm blood trickled down her neck. He dragged her along the dock, a human shield.

Locked outside the gate, with no other means of accessing the pier, the bikers watched helplessly as Otto and Lacey walked to the gangway and boarded Ava's Dream.

*Schoop, schoop, schoop, schoop, schoop...*

Otto looked up. A helicopter was approaching fast. On its fuselage, the emblem of the Federal Bureau of Investigation.

He rolled back the gangway. "Get below!" he yelled.

"No!" Lacey called out.

"THERE!" Chris said. He pointed to the yacht club parking lot. "Silver Range Rover." The agents watched as the drama unfolded on the dock below them.

Jordan looked down. "On the yacht," she said. "That's Lacey."

The water at the back of the vessel began to churn. Ava's Dream had started her engines.

The chopper swooped down hard and fast, taking a direct line of approach to the ship.

The yacht widened its distance from the dock. It started to turn, pointing its bow toward the open sea.

"Take us down!" Jordan yelled to the pilot.

"Copy that," the pilot replied.

The bird drifted downward toward the yacht.

Jordan removed her headset, slid open the helicopter door, stepped down onto the landing rail, called out. "Get me as close to that ship as you can!"

At the helm of Ava's Dream, Otto watched the helicopter circle the vessel in an attempt to cut it off. He gunned the engine. The mighty engines roared. The yacht surged ahead.

"He's trying to ram us," the pilot yelled. The helicopter pulled up sharply, rose into the sky.

Jordan yelled. "Again! Try again!"

The pilot swung the chopper down towards the ship once more. He opened the P.A. system. "Attention Ava's Dream," he said. The sound of his voice boomed through the public address speakers over the water. "This is the FBI. Shut down your engines. Prepare to be boarded."

Otto responded by zig-zagging the direction of the yacht, hard to the left, then to the right, port to starboard, successfully hindering the helicopter's approach.

"Hurry!" Jordan said.

"Get ready," the pilot yelled. "The further he gets from shore the choppier the water gets. With the rise and fall of the ship I'm only going to get one shot at this. Wait for my go, then jump."

"Copy that," Jordan replied. She held on tight to the side of the helicopter.

The chopper dropped quickly, veered in precariously close to the stern of the ship. "Now!" the pilot yelled. "*Go! Go! Go!*"

Jordan jumped from the helicopter. She landed on the rear deck of the ship, rolled, found her footing, rose to her feet, drew her weapon.

She looked up. Schreiber was gone.

With the helm now unmanned and with no one to steer

her Ava's Dream fell victim to the waves. Swells pounded the sides of the ship. Out of control, the vessel's course was being set by the sea itself.

Jordan crossed the deck precariously as the ship rose and fell.

In the distance, sheets of rain met the Atlantic.

Lightning flashed across an angry sky.

Thunder rolled.

Somewhere inside the ship, Lacey screamed.

# 55

DEGARIO AND ANTON followed Sam Chapman and the Hells Angels off the Sunrise Highway to Garney's Resort and Marina where two of the bikers blocked the entrance, two more the exit.

Sam and his men dismounted their machines.

Degario and Anton stepped out of the car.

Hearing their arrival, Henny Black looked back, called out. "He's got Lacey! They're on the ship!"

"God, no!" Anton said. He ran to the gate.

The men watched as Ava's Dream, out of control, criss-crossed the turbulent sea with the FBI chopper in close pursuit.

## 56

JORDAN ENTERED THE ship. Ava's Dream was massive, a luxury home on the water. Jordan cleared each room in search of Lacey. When she arrived at the master bedroom stateroom, she met the man she had been searching for.

Otto Schreiber stood behind Lacey, his knife to her throat. "You move, she dies," he said.

Jordan saw the blood on Lacey's neck, kept her gun trained on the killer. "It doesn't have to end like this, Schreiber," she said. "Let her go."

"You have no right to be here," Otto said. "Leave us, now!"

"You know I can't do that," Jordan replied. She made eye contact with Lacey, looked at Otto's wounded shoulder, then back at Lacey. Lacey understood what the agent was trying to tell her.

"We can all walk away from this," Jordan said, "but you need to put down the knife."

"No, no, NO!" Otto yelled. "She's mine! MINE! MINE! MINE!"

"You're injured. Let me get you the medical help you need."

"You need to leave!" Otto rested his forehead on his hostage's shoulder, looked down, and muttered to himself. "Mine... mine... make it real... make it real."

"You did it, Otto," Lacey said. "You succeeded. This is as real as it gets. What you need to do now is make it *right*."

"You can't leave me," Otto said. "You just can't."

"I won't," Lacey said. "I promise. Now put down the knife. Let me go. I promise I'll help you through this. I know how much you love me, but we both know this isn't right."

"I'm sorry," Otto said.

"I know you are," Lacey said.

"I should never have let it get this far."

"It's all right."

"I should have put an end to it long ago."

"You can do that now."

"There's nothing left for me."

"I'm here for you, Otto."

"So many have died."

"I know."

"We can still make it right, you and I."

"Otto..."

"There's still time," Otto said. He looked up. His hand tensed on the handle of the knife.

Lacey raised her head. "Otto, no," she said. "Don't do this!"

"Drop the knife, Schreiber," Jordan demanded.

Lacey's thoughts raced back to the limousine. The knock-out gas that had rendered her unconscious. The horrendous pain exerted upon her in the strappado in the dungeon. Bonnie Cole and the unthinkable mutilation she had endured at the hands of the madman who now held her tight within his grasp.

*The only enemy is fear,* she remembered. Better to die on my feet than plead on my knees.

Lacey drove her thumb deep into Otto's wounded shoulder. The killer cried out and lowered his arm but held fast to the knife.

Lacey continued the defense. She kicked up, drove her heel hard into Otto's groin, then grabbed his arm and spun around. In one smooth motion she turned the weapon on him, drove the knife deep into his gut.

She looked into the man's eyes, saw the shock, disbelief. "How's that for making it real, motherfucker?" she said. She pushed Otto aside, watched him fall to his knees.

Jordan rushed ahead, examined Lacey's neck. A light cut, minimal bleeding, but nothing serious. "Are you all right?" she asked.

Lacey looked down upon the fallen murderer. "Never better," she said.

"That was smooth," Jordan said.

"I have my moments," Lacey replied.

Jordan helped Otto to his feet. The wound was deep, serious. "He's losing a lot of blood," she said. "He needs to get to a hospital."

"That sack of human excrement?" Lacey said. "What he needs is another cut to match the one I just gave him."

"Probably," Jordan said, "but I can't let that happen."

"You actually want to save his life?" Lacey asked. "After all he's done, all the people he's killed?"

"No," Jordan replied, "I don't. But I don't have a choice. Neither do you. We need to get him out of here."

Lacey refused to move. "No," she said. "I want to watch

him die. For Bonnie and Melinda and Victoria. And for every other woman he's ever tortured or killed."

"You might still get your wish," Jordan said. "But I have a duty and a responsibility to save his life."

Lacey stared at Otto. He turned away. "Look at me you sick sonofabitch," she yelled.

Otto returned her stare.

"You don't deserve an ounce of compassion, you understand?" Lacey said.

Otto forced out the words. "You lied," he said. "Everything you said was a lie."

Lacey smiled. "Every last word."

"Let's go," Jordan said. "Help me get him up on deck. I need to stop the ship."

---

TOPSIDE, Jordan waved to the chopper.

Otto Schreiber was in custody.

Jordan handcuffed the killer, then leaned him against the side rail of the ship. "Stay with him," she told Lacey. "He may be wounded but don't take your eyes off him for a second. Got it?"

Lacey held Otto by the arm. "He's not going anywhere," she said.

"Good," Jordan replied. "I'll be right back."

The helicopter maintained a low but safe altitude above Ava's Dream.

Otto's breathing had become heavy, labored. "I'm dying, Lacey," he said.

Lacey shook her head. "No, you aren't. You don't get that luxury. I'll save your pathetic excuse for a life if I have to.

You're going to spend the rest of your life in prison. I'll see to that."

The knife remained lodged in Otto's stomach. Jordan had chosen not to remove it for fear the killer might bleed out and die.

Jordan opened the ship-wide communication system and called out to the chopper hovering above. "Schreiber's injured. Call it in. We'll need medical standing by when we arrive. I'll turn the ship around and take her back to port. Follow us in and set down at the marina."

The helicopter pilot responded over the loudspeakers. "Copy that, Agent Quest. Are you okay?"

"We're good," Jordan replied. "Ms. Chastain is fine."

"Copy. Nice work."

"You could have had it all, Lacey," Otto said. His wound had opened. Blood flowed freely now.

"Shut up," Lacey replied.

"Money, houses, cars... I could have given you the world."

"You're pathetic."

"All I ever wanted was to love you."

"You don't know the meaning of the word."

Otto looked overboard, stared at the choppy ocean. "These waters are dangerous, Lacey."

"You told me that before. So what?"

Otto smiled. "I should have learned how to swim."

The killer shouldered Lacey aside, rolled himself over the railing, then fell off the ship and plunged into the cold Atlantic.

"No!" Lacey yelled. She looked over the side of the ship.

Ava's Dream widened the distance between them. She called out. "Agent Quest!"

Jordan turned as she heard Lacey's cry.

"He's in the water!"

Agents Hanover and Penner and their pilot looked down as Schreiber gave himself to the sea.

Chris opened the door, grabbed the outside railing, prepared to jump into the ocean to rescue the drowning man.

Penner held him back, pulled him inside the chopper. "It's no use," he said.

"We have to try," Chris yelled.

Penner shook his head. "Forget it. It's too late," he replied. "Look."

In the water below, dozens of ghostly forms circled the murderer.

"Sharks." Chris said.

Penner nodded. "Great whites. This section of the coast is their main migratory path. Schreiber fell right into the middle of their breeding ground."

Otto's fall had opened the wounds in his stomach and shoulder. His blood flowed freely in the dark water. "Make it right," he said aloud as he looked up at Lacey from the roiling ocean. "Make it right... make it right... make it..."

The first contact with the deadly creatures pulled him under the water.

The gray water surrounding him turned black.

Fins broke the surface. Bodies thrashed beneath the waves.

Chris and Penner watched as the sharks pulled the killer's body apart, limb by limb, until he was no more.

Lacey looked over the railing of Ava's Dream and

watched her captor die a horrific death. In the moment, a great sense of relief overcame her.

Jordan turned the ship back towards port. Lacey joined her at the helm.

"You okay?" Jordan asked.

"I am now," she said. "Thank you, Agent Quest. You saved my life."

Jordan smiled. "I'd say you did that all on your own," she replied.

## 57

DEGARIO AND ANTON followed Sam Chapman and the Hells Angels into Garney's Marina as Ava's Dream pulled into her slip. The FBI helicopter set down in the parking lot. Special Agents Hanover and Penner exited the chopper and ran to the yacht. Penner wrapped his jacket around Lacey and escorted her down the gangway and along the wharf.

Chris walked with Jordan. "You see what happened to Scroll?"

Jordan nodded. "That was one hell of a way to go."

"Poetic justice, I'd say."

"He almost got away."

"But he didn't," Chris said. You stopped him."

"You mean we stopped him. It was a team effort."

"We didn't jump out of a helicopter, save the hostage, commandeer a yacht, and drive it back to shore. *You* did that."

Jordan smiled. "I have to admit the jumping out of the helicopter thing was pretty cool."

"It was," Chris agreed. "Just do me a favor."

"What's that?"

"Don't make a habit of it."

Jordan laughed. "I'll try not to."

"How's Lacey doing?" Chris asked.

"She's one tough customer. Scroll grossly underestimated her. In the end, he didn't stand a chance against her."

"Think we'll ever know how many women he killed?"

Jordan nodded. "One day."

Chris said, "Forensics is still processing the dungeon in the bookstore."

"They find more evidence?"

He nodded. "He's been at this for a very long time."

"We'll need to expand the investigation, look at unsolved homicides in other states," Jordan said. "I doubt someone like Scroll restricted his kill zone to New York City."

"I agree."

Penner opened the security gate. The agents watched as Lacey ran along the pier and fell into Anton's waiting arms. Chris stared at the reunited couple. "Now that is a very happy sight."

Jordan smiled. "Kind of makes it all worthwhile, doesn't it?"

"Better believe it."

"Any word on the trooper Schreiber attacked?" Jordan asked.

Chris watched the Hells Angels mount their motorcycles. The bikers revved their engines, then slowly exited the parking lot. "Our pilot was in touch with LifeFlight. Their paramedics were able to stabilize him on the flight to the hospital. He's going to be all right."

"Thank God."

Anton put his arm around Lacey, walked her back to the car. They stopped, looked back at the agents, and waved.

Jordan and Chris waved back.

In the parking lot, the helicopter's engines began to whine. Its rotors turned slowly. The chopper prepared for liftoff.

"It's been a long day, Jordan," Chris said. "You ready to go home?"

Jordan looked up. The storm was beginning to pass. The sun had returned. The air felt lighter, the day brighter. "Absolutely," she replied.

"Then let's get out of here," Chris said.

"Right behind you," Jordan answered.

# ABOUT THE AUTHOR

Gary Winston Brown is a retired practitioner of natural medicine and the author of the Jordan Quest FBI thriller series and other works of fiction. His books feature strong, independent characters pitted against insurmountable odds who are not afraid to stand up for those in need of protection.

*On the Author-Reader Relationship*

Getting to know my readers and building strong relationships with them is one of the best parts of being a writer. I put a great deal of effort into creating my books. My goal with every novel I write is to make it better than the last, earn your five-star review, and make your reading experience the best it can be.

I'd love to know what you thought of this book (or boxset). What did you like about it? Who was your favorite character? Did I keep you wanting to know what was going to happen next? What do you want to see in an upcoming novel?

Please subscribe to my monthly newsletter. I'll send you the series prequel, ***Jordan Quest***, for free as a thank you. Be sure to follow me on Amazon for updates on forthcoming books and new releases.

Follow me on Amazon

***Please Post a Review***

May I ask for your honest opinion. Did you like this book?

Reviews are the lifeblood to my work as a novelist. They mean the world to me. Long and fancy isn't necessary. What matters is your honest opinion. Did you enjoy this book? Did I deliver a good story to you? Rate it five stars and say a few words about what you most enjoyed about it. Or choose another rating. Your feedback is what matters. It's what makes me a better writer. And the better I can get at writing my books the better the reading experience I'll be able to provide to you.

**Why your review is so important**

I am a relatively new writer. I don't have a huge marketing machine or advertising department behind me like mainstream authors do to help build a buzz around my books and get them out in front of millions of readers.

But I do have *you*.

I am very grateful to have a growing following of loyal, committed readers who take the time to let me know what they think of my books. If you liked this book (or boxset) I would be extremely grateful if you would take a few seconds to post a review. It can be as long or short as you like. All reviews are appreciated and helpful to me.

Thank you!

*Gary*

## ALSO BY GARY WINSTON BROWN

**The Jordan Quest Thriller Series (in order):**

Intruders

The Sin Keeper

Mr. Grimm

Nine Lives

Live To Tell

Jordan's next adventure is coming soon!

Follow me on Amazon for the latest updates on new releases.

**Coming in 2021:**

The Matt Gamble thriller series

(vigilante justice, organized/international crime, assassination, spies, political).

The Vanishing (stand-alone thriller)

Made in United States
Cleveland, OH
15 April 2025